THE MENDELMAN FIRE

The Mendelman Fire is told by Humpy Botvinnik, the Demon accountant of Jubilee Street who could create a company for £12 and liquidate it for £5. He describes how his old friend Morris Mendelman plotted to secure his daughter's future, and how they learnt the vanity of human forethought—even if it's not inhibited by scruples—when it comes up against Nature. This is a racy short novel, rather in the vein of Mr Mankowitz's earlier *Make Me an Offer* but with a warmer sense of human relationships.

It is accompanied by two groups of short stories : *A Village Like Yours*, set in the Russian village from which Mr Mankowitz's grandfather came, and *Good Business with Sentiment*, a sparkling collection whose title is self-explanatory.

WOLF MANKOWITZ

THE MENDELMAN FIRE

ANDRE DEUTSCH

FIRST PUBLISHED JUNE 1957 BY
ANDRE DEUTSCH LIMITED
12–14 CARLISLE STREET SOHO SQUARE
LONDON WI
SECOND IMPRESSION JULY 1957
© WOLF MANKOWITZ 1957
ALL RIGHTS RESERVED
PRINTED IN GREAT BRITAIN BY
WESTERN PRINTING SERVICES LTD
BRISTOL

TO
MY FATHER AND MOTHER

ACKNOWLEDGMENTS

are due to the following newspapers and magazines in which some of these stories first appeared: *Chamber's Journal, Argosy, Time and Tide, Truth, The Complete Imbiber, Lilliput, The Atlantic Monthly* and *The Evening Standard*.

CONTENTS

I

THE MENDELMAN FIRE

II

A VILLAGE LIKE YOURS

III

GOOD BUSINESS WITH SENTIMENT

I
The Mendelman Fire

THE first time I did his accounts for Morris Mendelman he had a second-hand clothes shop in Cable Street. He was going out with Hettie at the time, Redhaired Hettie we called her, the daughter of Sam Finkin who had the grocery.

That time Mendelman wanted the accounts made up properly with debit and credit and balance carried forward and nett profit, so that Finkin would think it was worth Hettie's while to go to the Roxy with Morris and half a pound of chocolates every Sunday night. I ruled the paper out specially in red ink while Mendelman watched.

'Put in a couple more columns,' he told me. When it was finished it showed that Mendelman Clothes Co. was owed two hundred and eighty-three pounds by sundry debtors, owned assets valued at more than six hundred pounds, and there was forty-two pounds in cash into the bargain.

'Independent valuation,' Mendelman told Finkin.

Finkin liked the balance sheet very much, and in seven months Mendelman and Hettie were married with a house in Dollis Hill and a walnut bedroom suite bought and paid for by Sam. The wedding reception was at Margulies Dining Rooms by Leman Street. I had a table with Mendelman's brother, the one with the shirt factory. We had a long talk about whether it was better to be a company, and he asked me to call on him. The smoked salmon was piled so thick on the plates, the Master Tailors' Union could have made sandwiches for a week.

At that time it was fashionable to be a company, and my prices for making a company out of anybody were the lowest quoted. Nearly everyone you met was a company director. My clients would tell one another how their companies were getting on. One year I had six companies in Sclaters Street alone, but most of them lapsed and I arranged the liquidations. It wasn't that my clients had anything against being companies. It was disagreement between the directors. 'My co-director is nagging my life away,' they used to tell me. 'Ever since my wife became a director,' the chairman of Alf's (Pickled Herrings) Ltd told me, 'she won't stay in the house; every day she comes to the shop and helps me. I can't stand it.' The whilst I made a living. I could make a company for twelve pounds and liquidate it for five. The fees of Leo Botvinnik & Associates were the lowest ever.

On the other hand some of the companies I made did very well. Abrams & Berkoff Limited which became A & B (Girls-wear) was famous all over the country. United Metal Brokers, which I made for fifteen pounds including the name, would have been a great thing if Lippmann hadn't been silly about the income tax. And Mendelman Clothes Co. Ltd proved a good thing too. Morris always kept with me; though I say it, he could never have got on otherwise. His ideas about book-keeping were as clear as a plate of barley soup. When he started exporting to South Africa I used to send a clerk over to his warehouse every month. He was a good boy, that clerk, inter-B.Sc. mathematics, but even he said that for Mendelman's accounts you needed a slide-rule which hadn't been invented yet.

But Mendelman was never worried. He did some fairly large deals in army surplus uniform trousers and overalls for the Kaffir trade, but he never knew whether he was doing well or not. For him the only deal which meant anything was the one he was doing now. 'You still have fifty gross to sell, Morris,' I would tell him. 'But this is different,' he would say; 'there they are throwing at me; you want me to count like an old woman? Who counts?'

Morris was one of the first surplus men to sell by post. He started with a quantity of army jack-knives in a boys' paper. He wrote the advert himself.

Look, Boys!!!
A real jack-knife at last!!!
Combined tin-opener, screw-driver,
stone-remover, and three razor-sharp blades!
A shilling postal order brings you a pound jack-knife!!!

There was a little drawing of a knife with blades sticking out in all directions. After the jack-knives, he sold boots, denims, dubbin for football boots, handy metal boxes for bread or tools, stewards' drill jackets for light summer wear, and a special compass which fitted round the wrist and was suitable for scouts and guides. But mail-order was too slow for Morris. 'You want me to spend my life opening envelopes with sixpenny postal orders in them like a post-office clerk?' he said, and left his cousin in charge of the mail department while he went to South Africa to start a Kaffir business.

When Morris Mendelman went to Africa, Hettie already had Rosa. A wonderful picture they made together, both with deep red hair and white skin like marble, and blue eyes. Rosa was a year old, and Hettie cried every night for a month before Morris left, and for another month afterwards. Morris told her he would send for the two of them in a few weeks, but Hettie thought Africa was a big jungle full of lions and tigers and that if Morris went there he would get torn to pieces before he sold a single garment.

'Hettie,' Morris told her for the hundredth time, 'South Africa is just like London only hotter. They got big cities with good Kosher restaurants, and everyone is so busy making money selling clothes to the Kaffirs that even if a lion and a tiger was to come they wouldn't even see them. Anyway, everybody carries a gun and if that lion shows his nose, straightaway it is like a firework show at the Crystal Palace, a thousand bullets shoot him dead and teach him a lesson. What you want Hettie, I should spend my life loafing about Whitechapel Road saying "Good shabbos, Mr Pincus", while the world is passing me by like an old baigel-woman?' But Hettie went on screaming and crying and going back to her mother three times a week with Rosa in her arms.

After he had booked his passage, Morris came to me. 'Leo, make me an Africa company,' he said. 'You are the biggest company man in the world and for special business like this I must have a special company. I will write and tell you how I am getting on and you will make up some books, and Hettie and Rosa will come out for a nice holiday, and when we come back we will all be rich like Solly Joel and Barney Barnato and I will bring you a diamond as big as a fish-ball for a present.'

'But Morris,' I told him, 'who will look after the mail business, which is, after all, very good, and your only real money coming in? You are not Rothschild, Morris, you can't go to Africa and make a business straightaway. And to leave Hettie and your lovely baby.'

'Leo,' he answered, 'make me a company. Mendelman is also somebody and I am doing it for Hettie and Rosa especially, Rosa shouldn't grow up like we did, worrying, worrying, with no joy for living. You want me to be ashamed in front of my daughter when she grows up and tells me, "Daddy, why did you never send me to Cambridge college and let me learn to play piano and be a lady?" I couldn't stand it, Leo. Make me a company and good luck to everybody.' So I made Mendelman

Exports Co. (London) Ltd, and a few weeks later Morris left smiling, after kissing Rosa and Hettie a hundred thousand times and shaking his cousin's hand every time he said once more how well he would look after Hettie and Rosa.

What actually happened in Africa I didn't hear until many years afterwards. Morris wrote home every week telling Hettie he would send for her and Rosa soon, and what a wonderful country it was, and how well he was doing. He wrote to me a few times, telling me I should come out to a land where you didn't have to blow your nose all day long, and could I see his cousin and find out why the money he was asking for didn't come.

I never did like that cousin. He was a tall, broad man, very strong in the wrist, with a long, bony face all grey with small grey eyes and strong glasses, very quiet and religious, always wearing his hat when he ate, and walking everywhere, even ten miles, on the Sabbath day. Morris was a short, broad man, tending to fat even in those days, with bright brown eyes and his mouth always puckered up to laugh. He laughed until the tears came into his eyes, and with Morris you laughed too whether you liked it or not. The cousin never missed a synagogue service in his life, while Morris even on the Day of Atonement used to spend most of the time talking to someone outside about Charles Kingsley's *Hypatia*.

'What a marvellous book, you should read it. I learnt English from this book.' He had always a new book to be enthusiastic about. For a long time he told me every week to read Sir Humphry Davy's *Salmonia*. 'You read it and you think, all right, it's about how to catch salmon. But you're wrong. It is really about life. I will lend it to you, Leo.' His favourite book was Wolff's *Bokhara*, although Wolff was a proselyte. He would quote too from *The Vicar of Wakefield* in a sing-song—

'When a lovely woman stoops to folly.' But the cousin, although he was a very pious man and never read anything except Rashi's *Commentary* and the *Gems from the Talmud*, I could never like him.

I went to see him to ask why Morris hadn't received the money. He shook me by the hand and said I should sit down. He didn't pass the time of the day or ask me how things were. He said, 'Morris is very rash. The mail-order business is not so good. We have large stocks. Everyone is selling mail-order now. We are not getting many orders. Look.' And he showed me the orders for the past few weeks. The business had dropped to a few postal orders for lines which were mostly out of stock.

I wrote and told Morris, although I couldn't understand why the business had fallen off so quickly. It wasn't until I was going through Mendelman's accounts for that year and noticed that a firm called Excelsior Products had been buying very heavily from Mendelman Clothes that I realized what had been happening.

'But you have been selling these things at a loss,' I said to the cousin.

'What can I do?' he answered. 'I have to keep going and we have no capital, only this enormous stock, and only Excelsior will buy. We have no mail-orders to speak of. What can I do?'

I checked up on Excelsior Products Ltd and the next day wrote to Morris to tell him that his cousin had been selling Mendelman stocks for practically nothing to his own independent company. I think the cousin was transferring the mail orders to Excelsior as well. He was a very pious man, but I never liked him. I asked him how he could do this to Morris and still pray without choking himself.

When Morris came back from Africa he was very brown and had lost weight so that his suit looked as if it was slipping off him. For weeks afterwards he and Hettie would sit and look at one another by the hour with eyes full of wonder. It was as if they had both been in the shadow of death, and had seen death itself looking into their eyes, which now were full to the brim with love to make them forget. They watched Rosa stumbling about and Morris would keep picking her up and kissing her, and then Hettie would cry and kiss him again and again. And there they would stand, kissing one another and crying together, with Rosa between them laughing.

Morris wasn't interested in business all that time, and when I tried to talk to him about his affairs he would look at me as if he didn't understand what I meant and say, 'What difference does it make? You know, I think Rosa will be very musical. Yesterday she sang "Baa-baa black sheep" all through.' It was no use talking for the time being. The cousin had left Mendelman's as soon as he heard I had sent Morris the money to come back. The Exports company was bankrupt in Africa, and Morris had left it just in time. As it was, he had lived the last months working as a pot-boy in a public house and sleeping on the floor behind the bar. 'They gave me a wonderful free lunch on Saturdays,' he told me. 'Once a week I ate like a lord.' But he didn't talk very much. 'You should read a book called *With Buller in Natal*. It is very exciting,' he said.

Then one day he walked into my office in the Clerkenwell Road. His sunburn was beginning to wear off but he was still tanned enough for his eyes to flash like diamonds. They were certainly the only diamonds he ever got out of Africa.

'That lousy, filthy, rotten, bleeding, stinking bastard my cousin, he should drop dead, he should take a cholera, he should rot. You know what he has been doing? He has been robbing Hettie and Rosa. That's what.' He walked up and down the office.

'Did you just think of it, Morris?' I asked him. 'Didn't I write to you in Africa, that land you remember where nobody blows a nose, and tell you about that bandit? He has stolen your business.' He turned on me angrily.

'That I forgive. That I don't care. I can make another business. I will buy him and sell him a hundred times.' Then he told me that he had just heard from Hettie how she had called at the office more than once for money and the cousin had told her there was none. She had borrowed from a friend, a few shillings to buy food.

'And that hyena, he would steal the business and not spare her a few shillings to buy bread.' He wept hot tears of rage as he spoke. He screamed as if hot irons were tearing his flesh. He cursed and swore, and I sat there quietly until he had finished. What was there to say? He was full of hate and at the same time full of love. This way he left his hatred in my office and went back to Hettie with his love.

Within the year Mendelman's son Jacob, named for his dead father, was born. Mendelman was happy, although what with the worry and the fear and then, suddenly, so much love, like the sea running upon a small island of sand, Hettie was very weak.

It was a bad spring, that. Every week it suddenly broke into sunshine and the crocus bulbs in the graveyard we called Itchy Park began to peep through. Then a wind like a wet stone knife would cut through the air so that the sun fell away out of sight, and the paper in the gutters rattled like tin, and the crocuses were frozen stiff. A lot of people took the flu that spring. It was a special flu which left you in a couple of days if you were strong. But Hettie was weak, and it killed her. Then the baby pined for a day or two, taking no food, and one bitterly cold morning it stopped crying and Morris found it dead in the pink cot Hettie had bought, expecting another girl. May they find their place in peace.

II

ALL this was a long time ago, and besides, the past is finished. Better forget it and be done. Except no one ever forgets. It's a funny thing and you will perhaps laugh, but I think I could remember every company I made in those days when Morris was starting and I was a cut-price accountant. Although if you were to give me a thousand pounds, I couldn't tell the names of the firms I audit today. Of course, if suddenly the telephone rings and it is the income tax collector asking about this one or that one, what did they spend on advertising last year, I remember at once. But it doesn't mean the same thing. There is nothing for me to get excited about. I won't starve if I don't remember. Then it was different. Sometimes I had to collect five shillings advance fee from an old client. You might think that bad for business, except that everyone likes to own an accountant, more than a performing dog even. Also, believe me, they were saving money by employing Botvinnik & Associates.

You might have thought that after Hettie died Mendelman would have been finished, walking about like a man made of clay, not caring that there were stains on his jacket, not seeing anything except that face in which the eyes had gone like two hard-boiled eggs, not hearing anything except the whisper of a voice getting fainter every day. But no one can guess how trouble will take a man. The day after Hettie was buried he told me to put Mendelman Clothes into liquidation, and start forming Rosa Products. The creditors were paid off at six-andeightpence, and Morris was left with five hundred gross of soiled raincoats, small sizes, on his hands. They had been bought in Hettie's name before he went to Africa, and the creditors couldn't touch them. He sold the house in Dollis Hill and moved into my flat. Rosa went to live with his sister who had no children of her own. He wouldn't have anything to do with the Finkins because they had told Hettie from the moment she married him that he was mad, and she should wait and see, he would finish up in the gutter.

The first business Rosa Products did was to sell by mail-order five hundred gross of ladies' raincoats in bottle-green, nigger-brown, black, and bronze. Mendelman set about the new business like a man possessed by a dynamo. Rosa Products put out more adverts and handled more lines in the next twelve months than any three of Mendelman's competitors put together, including the cousin at Excelsior. Once that pig got the swill-bucket all to himself and gorged himself, he found out that you needed brains to fill it again. He went on offering lines that Morris had brought in, but every time he added something new he lost a little more stolen capital. He would try to sell woollen underwear in the summer and cotton frocks in the winter, and no matter how hard you pray, that is bad salesmanship. Morris kept an eye on Excelsior and one day he told me to ring his cousin up and say I had a purchaser for it.

'Listen, Morris,' I told him. 'I don't want to buy even a gold sovereign from your cousin for half-a-crown.'

'Phone him, Leo,' he told me. We bought it for the price of the stock, our valuation. Morris made me buy it in my name, and then told me to offer his cousin five pounds a week to stay on as manager. He accepted, and the next month Morris went over to the Excelsior warehouse, while I phoned through to explain that Mendelman was the final purchaser.

Morris walked straight into the office and sacked his cousin that day. When I saw him later, he told me about it.

'His face was grey like stone when he saw me, and I thought how much better he would look dead than Hettie. With him, death would be natural. But she should only have lived.' As a rule he never mentioned her name. I suppose he went with other women, but I don't think he cared whether they lived or died. With him, in his heart, it was only Hettie.

In the years that passed Mendelman worked often with Botvinnik & Associates. He made money, lost some of it, and made more. Then he took an order from some tin-pot South American government for thousands and thousands of bell-tents. At that time you couldn't give bell-tents away—they were all that old model, dark and only useful if you didn't want to breathe very much. How Morris arranged the deal, I don't know, but it made him. What did they do with all those tents, I wonder? The important thing is that Morris delivered them and was paid, and the money was good. Quite soon afterwards the government which bought the tents was liquidated, and the new government offered them back to Rosa Products for practically nothing. So Morris went over to South America to look into it, and when he came back he had sold the tents again to an American oil company. He also had orders in his pocket for the new government for a whole lot of other rubbish. After that if Mendelman walked down the street, he would pick up a five-pound note. Luck is like that. She has no time for the unlucky —but let her do you a favour once or twice, and she's got no time for anyone else. For Morris, for the time being, there was nothing she wouldn't do.

He bought his big house in Wimbledon in those days.

'I paid for it with rags. You want me to fill it with rags?' he said, when I suggested that perhaps he didn't need antique

Chinese silk embroidery for the curtains. He made that house, a rambling high Victorian villa, into a palace. He put in a big library first of all. He had a dealer in Charing Cross Road buying first editions for him all the time. He read them all and whenever he came across another book he liked he phoned the dealer and told him to get a first edition.

'That dealer is no good,' he told me one day when I was at the house looking at the books. 'I read a book by Ovid the other day and he can't find me a first edition. Very good book. You must read it. I will lend you my copy.' But as a matter of fact, Morris never lent anybody a book. Even when he was reading a book himself, he used to make a cover for it out of brown paper. He was very fond of books, but he spent a lot of money on other things too. He liked Chinese blue and white porcelain and had some large vases which I understood were worth a lot of money and extremely old, although they looked brand new to me and anyway too big for a side-board. But such things never interested me. I am more a man for science. I believe that in our lifetime it will be possible for men to fly to the moon. I used to tell Morris that men will discover new worlds in space.

'Tell me,' he would answer, 'what will they find there? More trouble. More misery. More things to fight over. More madness. The more flesh, the more worms. Will they live for ever if they reach the moon? Will they eat more than three meals a day, sleep in ten beds, read more than one book at a time? Leave me alone with your space and new worlds.' He was very reactionary in a lot of ways, and I told him so. 'I am a progressive. I am a mathematician, a scientist. You are not progressive, Morris, I am sorry to have to say. Mankind must move forwards, always forwards.'

'If you will excuse the expression,' he answered, 'kiss my arse. Mankind—what is mankind? I know a few men, a few women. But mankind—pardon me—is this something new? You made it up in your accounts, perhaps? You will make a limited company out of it? I don't see it. I don't feel it. I can't speak to it, love it, hate it, want it, not want it. It doesn't exist, your mankind, and your progress is a lot of horse-shit. There are always new ways of passing the time, but the time passes all the same. It is the same life, the same death, always, for ever. The more property, the more anxiety. We are men, for God's sake. Let us live men's lives. Not arithmetic.' How can you talk sense to a hot-head who has read too much and isn't properly educated into the bargain? We were friends, but except when we made up the books of Rosa Products, we never agreed about anything important.

All this time Mendelman's Rosa was growing up. She was fine, that Rosa, growing more like Hettie every time I saw her, but finer, with clear white hands and such a skin you could tell she had never washed dishes. She was away at some good school Morris read about somewhere, in the country, where they had an orchestra and kept horses, and important writers used to go and speak to them, although what they could have in common with a lot of children I don't know. I believe they did hardly any chemistry-with-physics at all at that school, although it was very expensive. In this way Rosa became a young lady. She was going to go to Cambridge, if you don't mind, with an allowance of five pounds a week. Five pounds a week, by my life—as much as we earned in a month at her age. She was studying music as Hettie had wanted, but in spite of all that expense, she couldn't even play the piano too well.

'Either I am mad,' I said to Morris one day, 'or something is wrong. Rosa tells me that *Madame Butterfly* is no good, and she can't even play the 'One Minute Waltz' well on the piano. What then does she study at Cambridge?'

'My dear Leo,' Morris explained to me, 'you are out of date. Today it is all different. You listen to a tune and you think, ah, a pretty tune. But today they are not interested.'

'So what do they want?' I asked him. 'Suddenly a bad tune is good?'

But Morris didn't worry what Rosa was learning, so long as she had the chance to learn whatever there was being taught.

'Let her live,' he said. 'That is the only thing.' So she became more and more educated, first coming to London to go to the Academy, and then running about abroad all over the place, Paris, Berlin, Madrid—so far you must go to hear music, the Albert Hall is not good enough.

Morris sometimes asked me to dinner when Rosa was home. He had a French cook-housekeeper at Wimbledon, with degrees, if you please, for cooking. She had a blue ribbon, two diplomas, another light-blue ribbon and a silver medal. 'Such a good cook doesn't grow on trees, you know, Leo,' he said. It's all very well, I told him. With so many ribbons she can dress her hair, but what sort of a stuffed neck can she make? But as a matter of fact, she was a good plain cook as well, and her stuffed neck was excellent. Her fishballs were very fine too, although my mother was also a great cook without having any ribbons. However, dinners at Morris's home were good, and when Rosa was home it was a banquet, nothing less.

After dinner Morris always asked Rosa to play for us. For some reason she was never very keen, and it wasn't the piano, because Paderewski never had a finer one. She played to us in the end, but to begin with you could tell her heart wasn't in it. Then Morris would go over to her at the piano and speak to her.

'You know, Rosa,' he would say, 'I am a pretty ignorant man. I don't know very much. But I know always whatever is in my heart, and if I haven't got a good understanding I can always say what I feel inside me. Sometimes what I feel is gone in a minute and other people say, "That Mendelman. He is not genuine". But when I am feeling it, it is true. If you don't feel any music, don't play it. Tomorrow you will again, and then you'll play marvellously. But now—what does it matter? Tomorrow is also a day and the piano won't walk and your fingers will be as quick, and your heart full of the music, and so you will play.'

Other times Rosa smiled at him and laughed at me and said, 'What shall I play you, Leo—"Softly Awakes My Heart"?'—because she knew that was always a favourite of ours. Then she was more like Morris' daughter. But those other times tears came into her eyes and she would say good night and go to bed. What was the use of pretending? She was different from Morris and her world was never ours. I knew it and Morris knew it, and Rosa worried about it and felt strange when she came back to us. But it was nothing to be sad about. This, I have always seen, is the way with children. They are suddenly grown-ups, strangers. You go to embrace them and they tell you, good morning, we haven't been introduced.

I am not a father myself, but I can imagine what it must feel like to see a fine girl grow up and think 'She is my daughter and a flower among women.' I can imagine how it would be to have a son and know that your name will go on being spoken in the world—have bad things said about it perhaps, but be mentioned by some with pride. Maybe to have one of your name do something great for mankind, something for which everyone will be grateful always. Botvinnik will be dead. His clients will go to other good firms, and if two of them meet they will say perhaps, 'Pity Botvinnik left no one to carry on. You know what we used to call him—the Demon Accountant from

Jubilee Street. But he is dead, old humpty-back Botvinnik. Is
that why he never married?' And it will be true, for I would
rather my hump remained a joke with my clients. It is not a
present for a woman I love. But this is neither here nor there,
except to tell you that I know how Mendelman loved his Rosa
and I was sad to see her grow up so strange to him, although
like him I was proud to see her so fine and well-educated.

And now I must come to the point where this story really
begins. Now that you know about Mendelman, and something
about his family and his business, I must tell you how he came
to me one day to tell me that he had once again lost his fortune.
Only this time he would not make it again. For he was going
to die.

III

In 1930 the whole world noticed that there was a depression
because a lot of very big people went broke and jumped out of
office windows and shot themselves. Also nearly everyone was
waiting for dole at the labour exchange, and business in the
East End was completely credit. The explanation of depression
is very simple. It is when the creditors who are giving credit
suddenly turn round and find there is nothing to eat in the
house. So they run over to their debtors to get a little on
account. Except that they can't because the debtors finished
their credit for last Friday night supper. Then everyone is
depressed, and that is depression.

But all this started before the big people shot themselves in
1930. Already in 1926 and 1927 a lot of small businesses found
there was nobody to sell anything to. And in August 1928 when
Morris came to tell me he had lost his fortune, a lot of people

were already scraping together enough pennies to buy a small pistol. Although in spite of that, I give it as my considered opinion that Morris had behaved very rashly. He should have taken more care than he did. But he could never be bothered with facts and figures. He thought that if you went broke it was because you had lost your nerve or your flair. You could talk to him about world trade cycles until you were blue in the face, he only laughed and told you the important thing was to live.

Rosa Products had long ceased to be just another small import-export business. Mendelman had become a manufacturer—one time it was novelties he made, then it was children's bicycles. Ever since he had been to Africa, and in spite of what happened to him there, he took every excuse to travel. On his travels he had picked up a contract to supply some special part for a sewing-machine company in France. It was only a small part, but it took a whole factory to make it. Mendelman took the contract for supplying the French firm, and it was going to be very big business indeed. He turned his entire capital over to it, put every penny he had into the new tools and machines. The factory was beginning to get its first order ready when the French company suddenly fell to pieces. There were trials afterwards and two or three went to prison, but a lot of people lost their money all the same. And Morris came to see me one hot afternoon in August 1928, months before the papers had it in headlines, to tell me his contract was worth nothing. He had thousands of sewing-machine parts which would fit no other sewing-machine in the world. Rosa Products was bankrupt. And he was going to die into the bargain.

That he was broke I could understand. It was serious, but from time to time you had to expect it. Also Morris was used to it, and had managed before, even in worse circumstances.

But that he was going to die—that was serious. Except it was impossible. Mendelman, a strong, healthy man not yet sixty, why should he die? I told him he was simply worried, he would be all right again as he was all right before. Anyone can go broke, and besides, the house and furniture were in Rosa's name. We still had two small companies with assets which couldn't be touched. He would start again, that was all. What was all this talk about dying?

He let me talk and then he sat down and wiped his forehead carefully. The air in the office was thick and heavy. You took it down into your lungs but it was no more use than the air you already had down there. The heat hung on your skin like a blanket, and it tasted stale, like the air of a bedroom with no windows.

'Look, Leo,' Mendelman said at last. 'You are my friend, my old friend of many years. You know me, you knew Hettie, you know Rosa, you have watched her grow up. I am not making a joke. I will be dead before this time next year.' He laughed. 'Perhaps this will prove it to you,' he said. 'I just paid a heart specialist five guineas to tell me. And other doctors have told me the same for less money.' I asked him if they could be mistaken. Even a specialist could make a mistake.

'Leo,' he said, 'this is not mathematics. This is an old worn-out heart that is no good to anyone. If it was a car-engine you would throw it away. It is finished.'

'But die—why die?' I asked, and I could feel there was no blood in my face, and I thought as I spoke that if you love a man this is how you feel. 'Surely with modern medicine they can keep you alive—you can retire—lead an easier life. You will live for years more. Why die?'

'Leo, my friend,' he said, 'a man dies when he has to—not when he wants to. I will do my best to live, I assure you. But I think they are right, and that I will die no matter how hard I try not to.'

What could I do? I am not an emotional man, but this was a great shock to my system and I couldn't speak because tears choked me whenever I opened my mouth. I just opened my mouth three or four times without anything coming out.

So I sat quiet and listened to the most dishonest proposition which has ever been put to me in my life.

'I want you, Leo, my friend,' said Mendelman, 'to listen to me till I finish—whatever I say, listen. Sit quietly there, light a cigarette. Maybe when I finish speaking I will drop dead. The heat when I go into the street will be too much. I will die in the Underground. So listen. Maybe I am already a man speaking from the grave. This is what I have to say.

'We are friends, Leo, for thirty years. We were boys together, running after the girls, having big ideas, working, hoping, dreaming. If one man ever can know another man, you know me—I know you. Good. All this is very good. Good things have happened. Bad things as well . . . although sometimes the good things turn out not so good, and the bad things could have been worse. What does it all mean? I don't know. Why? Because one minute it means one thing, and the next minute something different. This is what life is, and for this kind of monkey-business there is no accountant. At the end it is neither profit nor loss. At the close of business there is nothing—no more bargains, no more arguments, no more presents for everybody, no more baked *kishka* to eat, no more lemon tea, no books, no kisses. In a word, nothing. That's why a man must care about life and living things. Most of all, he must love the life he has made. That life is not what I have been and done. It is my child.'

Mendelman paused and lit a cigarette from his case. He

smoked the old Russian ones in yellow paper, and he held the match between his brown fingers for a few seconds while it burned, drawing on the cigarette in the exact centre of his lips, and looking at me with pursed-up eyes. It was his last speech maybe, and Morris was always a speech-maker. He was going to make it good. Already I was forgetting everything else and getting ready to enjoy a real Mendelman speech, for he was a great talker, especially when you remember he was not even properly educated. When I was at Toynbee Hall studying, he was already selling clothes. But how he could talk, that Mendelman! He drew another deep breath through his cigarette, and blew the smoke out in a long, thin cloud. Then he spoke, underlying the points with the index finger of his left hand.

'Why do you think that everyone smiles when they look at a child? Is a baby funny? Does he say something to make you laugh? You smile at a baby because in your heart you are saying, this baby will live when I am dead. My life will be in his life, a little bit, whoever he is, whatever he becomes. And you smile because you are happy that life will go on. And with your own child, how much more true is this? The man who does not love his children is dead and has never lived, and they too will never live, and without love the whole world dies. The only men who should be punished are those who do not love. And already they are punished, for not to love is to tear your heart and your liver to shreds, like a wild dog in your stomach, terribly painful. Such men die screaming for another life, another chance. It is for them a heaven must be made, so that they leave a real hell behind them and pass into a world in which there is no more pain, no wild dogs.

'But I love my child, and so when I die I will not even notice it. I will not be thinking about it, only about living things, my things which still live on and on, always, somehow. Yet although they will always live somehow, a father must try to give his children every chance. He must help them, even if he is dead, to get on with the main business—to make living good, better than his life, so that the life of their children may be better again, and so better and better until from the first moment until the last, life is a joy and, as my father (may he rest in peace) used to say, a pleasure to God.

'Now Leo, you and I know that this needs money. This is the meaning of money, to smooth the way, so that a man's life is not wasted in always worrying, no time to read a book, to talk to friends. Who wants such a life? But how can there be a better life for men if they are poor? Poverty is hateful and terrible. We have known it before—no fire to keep us warm, no food but thin cabbage soup, no laughter in the house, only the endless nagging of tired women and the anger of defeated men. Against that existence I have made money, and given my child whatever she could be given, even you say sometimes, too much. She will think nothing of money, you say. She will not care that it must be worked for. Good. She will be better for that. Rosa will have time to find out about better things, time to run after great ideas. Maybe she will catch them. Who knows? And if not, at least she would have tried, and this must be good. As for making a living—if he has to, any man will find a way to do that. And he will find a better way if he knows only about the best things. This anyway, is what I have always thought.' Mendelman paused again, looking sad for a moment, and then laughed. 'But,' he said, 'such a kettle of fish is life that now, all of a sudden, not only am I going to die, but I am going to be bankrupt as well.'

He laughed again as if he enjoyed the idea, and perhaps he did, because Morris could talk himself into anything. The trouble with a good salesman is that when he is selling some-

B

thing he thinks it is the best thing in the world. Mendelman was the finest salesman I ever knew. Whatever it was, he could sell it. You took it home and opened it up thinking it was a new life in a brown paper parcel he had sold you, and when you found it was only a couple of khaki shirts, you thought, Well, even if it isn't a new life a couple of shirts is always handy, I could even make a profit on them. And you wanted Mendelman to sell you things again—always a new world going reasonable, always something you could use. This is what makes a good salesman. He must want to give you something which he thinks will do you good. The money you give him is just what he needs to go on living, to go on buying, to go on selling something to you for your own good. The bad salesman is the man who doesn't care, so long as he gets your money. And what good is he? Will you buy from him again? Let him drop dead, you will walk over his body, the jackal.

'Yes, Leo,' Mendelman continued, 'this is certainly the end of the business. Not only one end. Both.' He smiled, and then suddenly the smile was gone. 'But do you think I will do this to Rosa?' he asked. 'You want me to die and let her think her father a fool and a failure? You want her to remember me from the depths of misery? Even if I was dead, my heart would burn. No, Leo. I can't do it, not even for you, my oldest friend. Not for the world.'

He crashed his fist down on my desk so that the ink-well jumped, and I replied, a little startled, 'All right, Morris, all right, I wouldn't dream of asking you to do such a thing. You think I'm inhuman?' But still he glared at me as if I wasn't his friend.

'No, Leo,' he said at last, 'I have a plan.'

It was always Mendelman's way. He talked to you about life. He frightened you a little bit, he made you cry maybe, he shouted at you. And then, at last, he had a plan. It was always his way. And there are, I think, worse ways of doing business.

IV

THIS was Mendelman's plan.

Rosa Products would have to go into liquidation when the French sewing-machine company folded up publicly. The assets of Rosa's were its machines, useless for anything except the one special job, its stock of sewing-machine parts, office furniture and so on and so forth. The lease of the factory premises of course, but in 1929 who was starting factories? The whole lot was worth nothing but its breaking-up price. The factory could stand there with a big sign up saying *For Sale*, and fall to pieces waiting for a buyer.

But it would take a couple of months before the French company was finished. And maybe a couple of months more before Mendelman's firm need go into liquidation.

Now supposing, only supposing with these new machines and electric dynamos and so forth, there was to be a fire at Rosa Products, and the whole lot went up in smoke. What would it be worth then? Fifteen thousand pounds fire insurance.

'But Morris,' I told him, 'that money would belong to the company when it was liquidated, would be used to pay off the creditors. And anyhow, a fire would be nice, but what can you do? Pray for lightning to strike?'

Of course, Morris agreed; the money was the company's. But at the same time, wasn't he the company, and couldn't he draw the money before publicly liquidating the business?

'Morris,' I told him, 'you are being silly. They would get

that money back from you if they had to take it out of your pocket with torture, murder and assassination. What is all this nonsense? You, an experienced business man. I'm surprised.'

'Of course,' he agreed. 'Only I wouldn't have the money. Rosa would have it.'

'Now you are even more ridiculous,' I told him. I was beginning to be angry at all this nonsense. 'They would get it from Rosa too. They should worry if your child starves. They want their money and they will get it.'

'They won't get it, Leo,' he answered. 'It will be legally Rosa's money. No one will touch it. Listen again.'

And he described an even more terrible plan. Professionally speaking, I have never heard such a shocking suggestion in my life. Listen to this and blush.

Mendelman was going to write a whole lot of letters to everyone he knew, all people who knew Rosa. In the letters he was going to say that Rosa was a woman of low morals, a loose-liver, no better than a harlot. It was terrible. And Morris was laughing as if he was at the Palladium, and by some chance hadn't heard the joke before.

Then we would arrange, he said, with our old friend Weiss the solicitor for Rosa to sue Mendelman for libel and defamation of character. And Mendelman would settle out of court for fifteen thousand pounds. He would pay it in cash, and then, no matter what anyone could say or do, Rosa would be provided for.

'Could it be more legal than that? Can you say it isn't a good idea?' Mendelman asked, slapping my shoulder.

'Not only is it a brilliant idea,' I told him, 'it is completely *meshuggah*. You are mad as a hatter. You had better lie down. I have got a headache myself.' But I knew Mendelman was serious, and all I could hope was that he didn't want me to start

the fire for him. In my profession, after all, there are certain
ethics.

I was like the little man in the old story. Two big men are
having an argument in the middle of the street. The little man
stands between them. They become violent. One shouts. The
other shouts. They raise their hands against one another. They
scream at one another. All the time the little man looks from
one terrible face to the other terrible face, his eyes getting bigger
and bigger. Suddenly he can't stand it any more. 'Leave me
alone for God's sake!' he shouts. 'Haven't I got troubles of my
own?'

I wanted Mendelman to leave me alone. But I knew he
wouldn't, although, thank God, he didn't want me to do anything except go and see Rosa and explain the arrangement to
her. 'You mean to say,' I said, 'you can bear to write such terrible things about your own lovely child? It is a monstrous
thing to do.'

'You are not an artist, my Leo,' he said. 'I am not saying
anything about my child. I am making a drama, a story, and in
this story there is an old dying man called Mendelman and he
happens to have a daughter called Rosa. That is all. You are
only upset because it is such a good story you think it is true
when you hear it. That is how a story should sound. But it has
nothing to do with life. It is not my Rosa I am talking about.
I am making a business arrangement, that's all.'

That night what with the worry of Mendelman and the heat
of a long day, my hump was like an aching furnace. I always
sleep on my left side with one pillow under my head and a
larger pillow under my shoulder to stop me turning onto my
back in my sleep. Years ago I worked this out as the best way,
and always it has been good, and I have slept as well as you
might yourself. But this night I twisted and turned, pushing the

pillow about. The hump was so hot I couldn't breathe from the heat in the bed. My head was full of figures turning round and round very fast, and I was trying to stop them so as to add properly. But they wouldn't, so I got up to make a cup of tea.

While I waited for the kettle to boil, the figures in my head still turned round, but slowly this time. When I added them up they came to precisely fifteen thousand. That Mendelman, how often had I worried about his figures? How often had I woken up and straightaway thought, 'Mendelman's books today.' And yet, what else did I have to do? I poured myself a cup of tea sitting at the table, my dressing-gown round my shoulders and over my back. It didn't ache so much now, but it was still hot, so I let the dressing-gown slip onto the floor.

I drank tea and thought that a man is born from an accident maybe. A young couple, hot and clammy in the darkness, their eyes half-closed with wanting one another, their breath heavy and quick, their hands groping in the night for something certain. What do they know about life? What do they care? They want one another, they want to make love and then sleep quietly. They get up in the morning and the woman is thinking that she must make breakfast and clear up and do the shopping. The man is thinking he must hurry to the office and will Rosenberg ring today and yes he will take the lot at ten per cent less. Yet though they hardly look at one another, though they do not know it, they have carried another life into being. Quietly, quietly, life is beginning again, knowing nothing of them as they know nothing of it. And so she goes shopping and he goes to wait for Rosenberg to ring. And later on a man is born.

What gives it meaning? Maybe this little man is a messiah the world waits for. He may be the inventor of a different kind of internal combustion machine, using air as fuel, making mankind rich and happy. He may develop a new language for all men, invent a perfect accounting system, be the first man to step on Mars, discover a drug to end evil. Or he may be just another man who waits for Rosenberg to ring, and sometimes in the night gropes, hot and breathless, for another human body in the darkness. How should we know what it means?

In all the years I knew Mendelman I learnt enough about him to know that he was a groper—a man born to make one try after another, make a company, lose a company, sell something, buy something, on and on. A man made to go on trying and to have children. He was a mistake, but that was what he had to do. I was a mistake, perhaps a mistake my mother never enjoyed, one she never wanted to make. I don't want to know. Mendelman's children, somebody else's children, what did it matter? I was glad that one of them was so close to me, become like my own. I was going to do something for Rosa, for her good and no other reason.

Gradually I began to feel very pleased with myself; my head stopped going round, and my hump stopped aching. When I went back to bed, I put the pillows right and lay down: I fell asleep at once and had no dreams.

V

I WAS going to see Rosa. She was living in a hotel in Paris. Imagine. Leo Botvinnik in Paris.

I didn't like the idea of going at first, but when I got used to it I felt quite excited. From all accounts Paris was a fine city. Mendelman told me it was very nice, everybody sitting in cafés all day drinking sweet wines and talking, with very lovely buildings and a lot of monuments and statues, and the wonderful smell in the streets of beautiful women with perfume and delicious food cooking everywhere. 'You will come back with a wife, I think, Leo,' he said. 'Those French women are very fine girls. Be careful.' He teased me as if I was a schoolboy, and me two years older than him.

My chief clerk arranged all the papers, and the ticket, and wrote down the trains in a notebook, with Rosa's address.

'How will I speak to everyone, Morris?' I asked.

'I have been all over the world,' he replied, 'and even if you can't speak the language you can always make yourself understood so long as you know what you want. Don't be a baby, Leo, a grown man like you. Also, you could get a small book and learn French. It would be useful to you. There are very fine books by Frenchmen. *Candide* is very funny, and *Penguin Island* is also good. You must always be willing to learn, so don't make difficulties. Just go and tell Rosa what is to be done.' So I went.

I was sick twice on the boat. The second time it was terrible. I wanted to die. I was having a nice conversation with a traveller, a man with a goitre, very intelligent, in the bar, and drinking a brandy to settle my stomach. We were talking about whether there was human life on any of the other planets, and I was explaining that on Venus men would have to live on ammonia gas instead of air, while on Mars there was very little oxygen in the atmosphere. Then I felt my face go white and I said excuse me and rushed down to the gentlemen's lavatory, and got there just in time.

When at last the sea stopped throwing me up and down like a rubber ball and the boat was coming into port, I could hardly wait to get out onto dry land. How do sailors live in such conditions? Up and down, up and down. The sea is for fish, although steam is a great invention and no doubt ships were even worse before the gyroscopic balance was invented. They are still terrible.

It was no trouble on the train. They took my brief-case away and wrote in chalk on it and gave it back to me. The train was standing right there waiting, so good is the service. I found my seat, looked out of the window for a while and then fell asleep. When I woke up I was very hungry, but it was nearly Paris so I waited. I was going to spend the night at a hotel Morris knew. In the morning I would go by taxi to Rosa's hotel and speak to her. Rosa didn't know I was coming, but early in the morning I would be sure to find her in. After I had explained things to her I would catch a train, and come back—God help me—on the boat at night. But maybe if I slept it wouldn't make me ill again. This time I had a little cabin booked. I saw one coming over, very nice and comfortable. I would take three aspirins and drink a couple glasses of brandy very quick and sleep through it, please God.

The Paris station is very like Liverpool Street, except everything is different and in French. Even the lavatories have *Hommes* and *Femmes* on them. I learnt a little bit of French studying the advertisement posters which are brighter than in London. You know what the French for motor-car tyre is? *Pneu*. I looked it up in my book. *Pneu*. You could never guess it in a million years.

I got a taxi and said, 'Bitte, hôtel ici,' and showed the driver the name Morris wrote down for me. He understood after a while, and drove me there. If I spent a few months in Paris, with my mathematical training and interest in scientific things, and a language is after all a kind of science, I would pick up French very quickly.

At the Hôtel Weinberg it was easy. Even the porter spoke yiddish—with a foreign accent but at least you could understand it. I met Mr Weinberg the proprietor, who asked me how terrible business was in London. He showed me to a room on the first floor with a double bed, very comfortable, and said I could have dinner just when I wanted it. I might have been in my own home, except, of course, outside everything was French, the cars, the clothes. As a matter of fact, I did notice that the French ladies looked very attractive and smart.

I had dinner with Mr and Mrs Weinberg at their own table, but I didn't talk very much with the lady as she couldn't speak the mother-language. But Mr Weinberg asked a few questions for her. It seemed she was very fond of Mendelman, who she said was very spirited and full of charm—like she was talking about a dancer at the Russian ballet. Dinner was chicken soup with *creplach*, very delicious, some good *hamische* fish, and roast veal, and then suddenly *tzimmis* and little golden potatoes and lettuces with vinegar and oil, all a bit different from home. But I followed the Weinbergs, eating everything separately with the same knife and fork, like a real Frenchman. Mrs Weinberg, a lady about forty-five, buxom with bright eyes and a pretty mouth, taught me a few French words, like thank you and please. Afterwards I played *club yoss* with Weinberg until late, winning two hundred francs. I drank a glass of wine with my dinner and another glass afterwards. When I went up to bed, people were still walking up and down the street. Those Frenchmen don't care about sleeping.

In the morning some rolls and butter and coffee were brought to the door. I shouted out they should leave them there, then put on my dressing-gown, unlocked the door and brought the tray in. After breakfast, Mr Weinberg called me a taxi and told the driver where to take me. In no time at all, I was going to see Rosa.

But now, after it had all been going so smoothly except for

the boat, it suddenly became difficult. At the hotel they didn't understand what I was talking about. I wrote down Rosa's name on a piece of paper and pointed to it and said 'Où est la?' and they said she had left two weeks before to go to another hotel. They wrote the name down for me and talked a lot with the cab-driver who was a boy Weinberg had told to look after me. They talked loudly, and I thought, hello, it's going to be trouble, but it blew over and Moishe the driver said he would explain to me on the way over to another hotel.

It appeared that Rosa had stayed at this hotel for a long time, but that now she had a flat.

'Very nice,' I said to Moishe.

'Who knows?' he answered, driving fast. He nearly knocked people over three or four times, he didn't stop for lights or sign what he was going to do—a real Frenchman. I was glad when the drive was over, I can tell you. On the way we passed what must have been the biggest fountain in the world, making even Trafalgar Square look small.

At the address we found a note saying in French that Rosa was having breakfast round the corner. How could she know I was coming? And why leave me a note in French? It was very mysterious.

We drove round, and I got out of the car. The sunshine was very bright now, and I blinked for a while looking up and down the tables on the pavement outside the café. Then I saw the sun on her red hair shining like copper. I called out to her, 'Rosa, Rosa, look who has come all this way to see you!' She looked up at once.

'Uncle Leo!' she cried. 'What are you doing here?' She stood on the pavement in the sun, her skin very white, in a pretty green dress, looking so beautiful that I was very proud everyone should hear her call me uncle, even if they didn't understand English. She was with a man, but I didn't notice him until she bent over for me to kiss her cheek which now was pink with a blush. Then I sat down and we asked one another questions for a while. How was her father? What a long time it had been! What was she studying now? And so on and so forth as people do when they are a bit uncomfortable. At last I got to the point.

'Rosa,' I said, 'I must speak to you very seriously, and alone, if this gentleman can be left for a while. Perhaps it would be best to go back to your flat.' She spoke in French as good as a native to the man, who stood up and bowed when we left. In the car I remarked:

'A very nice young man. Nicely brought-up. You can tell without speaking to him.' But she didn't answer. Maybe she thought it was none of my business, and of course she was right.

The flat was high up in a narrow house, and when I got my breath back from climbing about a hundred thousand stairs, I carefully explained what had to be done, and laughed as I showed her the draft letter Mendelman intended to send around. 'My daughter Rosa has broken my heart. She is no better than a whore, though it kills me to say it. God forgive her.' While I laughed like a jackass to make her feel at ease, poor Rosa turned very pale. Then she cried as if her heart would break, while I still sat there like an idiot telling her again and again that her father didn't mean it—it was only a technicality so that he could provide for her. I hadn't told her yet that Mendelman was, without technicalities, going to die. She went on sobbing, her whole body heaved as if breaking in pieces.

'Rosa,' I said at last—for there was no other way—'Rosa. Your father is dying. Soon he will be dead. He wants only to help you. Try to understand and help him so that he may die happy. You are clever, you know how things are in this life. Try to help. Be sensible.'

Then, like a woman, when I gave her something to cry about, she stopped crying and stared at me with red eyes out of a grey face.

'Tell me,' she asked quietly, 'what is wrong with him? What can be done for him? Something must be done for him. I must go home.' She stood up as if to go home at once.

I was sitting in a low armchair and what with my hump and my belly it takes me longer to get up than most people. Rosa stood with a window behind her, her figure like a silhouette. She had always been a slim girl, but now she had lost her figure a little. Suddenly I knew why she wept. I cursed myself and Mendelman's schemes together.

'Rosa,' I said quietly. 'Rosa. I think you are going to have a baby. Is this so?' She turned her face towards me and nodded, her lips pursed up tight.

'But I love him, Uncle Leo,' she cried. 'I love him so much. I am glad to have his child. It is right for me. Only how could father say such things? Could he know? Tell me, Uncle Leo, do you think he knows, and that's why his heart is weak?'

Of course not, I told her, he isn't a magician. It was just his luck he happened to think of such a thing, such a ridiculous scheme, which he would never have thought of if he hadn't been sure it was impossible. Furthermore, what was there to cry about? All right, the baby was started a little early, but that can happen as well. She could get married and then everything would be fine.

It is my luck to say the wrong thing in such circumstances. I should be a diplomat, so carefully I put everything. Anyone else would have known that she was crying not because she was pregnant—sooner or later most women expect that. She was crying because the man—that man she was having breakfast with—was already married.

'But he loves me,' she said. 'We would marry if we could. But his wife is a terrible woman. She hates his work—he is a wonderful composer, Uncle Leo, really wonderful—she hates me. She hounded me out of my hotel. She hates every decent, wonderful thing, everything that makes him happy she hates.' And in the same vein for a few minutes.

It was for this man that she stayed in Paris. Her work? She didn't care about her own work. She only wanted to help him, to do what she could for his genius, help him as a wife helps a husband, as a woman helps a man and an artist.

It was a whole performance, I can tell you. You wouldn't have thought a Cambridge girl could be like that. Which only goes to show that education is a waste on a woman. As soon as they fall in love with a man, it all goes to hell. But it wasn't for me to tell her how to live. What do I know anyway? Maybe he was a genius. Maybe it was right for her to have his child. Maybe they would get married. Although when he got married before wasn't it the same thing, all this love and for ever business then as well? But this is the sort of thing you must never say to a woman. This time it is always different. Thank God, I remembered and didn't argue with her.

But so far as Rosa was concerned, Mendelman's plan was a washout. Now all I had to do was to go back and tell him about Rosa, and—God forbid—he would have heart-failure on the spot. What was I supposed to do—The devil take me for a certified lunatic to start with Morris in the first place. It was a mad idea from the start, and now I would go mad as well, not being able to tell Morris why it couldn't be done this way, and having to find some other way of making sure Rosa's bastard had a good schooling. Excuse me putting it this way, but I was very upset.

Anyhow, we went back to the café where Rosa's friend was still sitting looking very sad. When he saw that Rosa had been crying he turned on me with an angry face, and said something very quickly to Rosa. She answered him, and with a lot of hums and haws he said to me, 'This is a terrible thing. Her father is to die?' So she at least had enough sense not to tell him about Mendelman's plan.

We had lunch together. They were, I could see, very much in love. When their eyes met he grew more handsome and she looked more beautiful. They loved one another all right, and so, I suppose, it was certain that they would have a baby sooner or later. Although you would think that with a Cambridge education it might be different. But no, women are alike in that. As a matter of fact, no one has ever mentioned it, but I am sure Hettie herself, even with her strict background, I think even Hettie was a little bit pregnant when she married Mendelman.

I don't know what you do when you have to think something out carefully. Some people eat a big dinner and go to sleep as if they could dream up an answer. Some pull their noses and play chess, some go for a long walk as far as Finsbury Park perhaps. I knew a man who used to read algebra whenever there was anything on his mind. For my part I walk round the room whistling. I don't think about what I am whistling, but if I should happen to notice, a hundred to one it will be an aria, and this isn't surprising because I am particularly fond of grand opera. I was finishing my coffee in this little restaurant we went to for lunch, a nice little place not unlike Soho, and Rosa was talking to Albert, as his name turned out to be, only with the 't' not pronounced, when suddenly I noticed that I was singing under my breath, 'All the Flowers Awaken'.

'Did you say something, Uncle Leo?' Rosa asked. I cleared my throat and spoke to the two of them, chattering there like a couple of sparrows with nothing to worry about except which direction the cat was coming from.

'I think the time has come, Rosa and Albert'—and I said it with the 't' because this was no occasion for flighty nonsense— 'the time has come for us to consider what is to be done. What are we going to do?' I repeated, to bring home the point.

Rosa looked as if she was going to cry again, and Albert looked down his nose as if he would rather make jokes with Rosa. But it was no good. All that nonsense there is a time and place for. And there is a time for action as well. I was going to bang my fist on the table, but I thought it would draw too much attention, and it was a small table anyway. I went straight into a consideration of our problems.

'The point is this,' I said. 'This is the point. You, Albert, have to get a divorce at once, and then you have to come home with Rosa and get married.' To hell with it, I thought, and I really did bang my fist on the table. All the plates shook, and everyone looked round at us, and Rosa's eyes were like saucers, but I didn't care. There is a time for action. This was it.

A pity I am so quick to suggest what is good for people. You should have heard the talk, the tears, the argument this way and that. The whilst I know it will be Botvinnik, chartered accountant and man of action, who will have to see Albert's wife and come to suitable arrangements.

And that was how it turned out. Albert took Rosa off to kiss her better, because though kissing causes the trouble in the first place, people still go on believing that it can also make everything well again. And I am left, I can't say carrying the baby, but anyhow with another slip of paper with the name Mme Jocaste Barré, rue Lepin 16. All I have to do is find the address, speak to this woman and tell her she should give Albert a divorce at once, because our Rosa wants him. How could she refuse? Such a reasonable request, it happens every day and Rosa being such a nice girl, what wife would object?

I could kick myself, such a complete fool I am for getting into places where I have no business, such a busybody I am, such a bighead. My father—God rest his soul—used to tell me, 'Every man has his own proper measure of trouble; but you will have a little bit more, because everyone else will kindly give you a piece of theirs, such a nice fellow you are.' He was right except that I am not such a nice disposition, only I get bored because everyone else is worried and I am getting on with my work, and life is very dull if there isn't something to worry about. But believe me, you don't have to encourage people to part with trouble. You hardly know them before they are crying and asking your advice and the next thing you know you are driving out to see their wives to ask them for a divorce, Rosa would like their husbands.

Moishe drove me out to this rue Lepin in the afternoon. His business must go to hell because he hung about waiting for me all day long, and twice I saw him refuse to take a fare, smoking cigarettes and reading a sports paper. When we went to lunch I thought he would go, but he was outside waiting for me. He said when I came out of the restaurant with Albert and Rosa, 'So, what now?'

I would like to have been able to tell him.

VI

THAT Albert, he had certainly worked his way up from nothing. Here he was, engaged, in a manner of speaking, to our beautiful Rosa. And here I was, trying to talk business to his wife, who was absolutely no class at all, except such a low class I wouldn't like to be seen with, although in the way of business it goes without saying there is no class distinction.

To such a woman as this, Albert (with or without the 't') was tied—with a great bush of black hair, greasy, knotted, wearing trousers (not a garment for a nice sort of girl) and gipsy ear-rings, not at all inappropriate because she had these dark features like Carmen, and was so nervous, smoking the whole time, I expected her to start dancing the habañero any minute.

It turns out, in spite of looking so foreign, Albert's wife is English, from a very nice family in Croydon. She comes to Paris, she tells me, to learn the painting business. What with girls coming to Paris to learn music, and painting, I am surprised there are still girls left in England. What is more, I don't care what you say, all this Boheme business is very nice in the opera, but it's a different matter when it happens in your own home. Still, let Jocaste's father send his accountant to Paris to get her out of trouble. I have enough problems with our own Rosa.

I didn't mince words. I said straight out to the lady, perfectly frankly, 'I am representing a big legal concern in London. There is a small matter of a will. But first I must ask you something.' I could see from this studio, filthy dirty, the stove out, the table covered with used plates, that 'Jo' (as she signs the paintings stacked up against the wall) is not what you might call a popular painter. I decided to work in the dark on the proposition that a little money doesn't come amiss, even if it sometimes means selling a husband. In this, human nature is the same for artists and others. Jocaste was straightaway interested. As soon as I mentioned a will, she started to smoke very fast till smoke came out of her ears and it looked like her hair was suffering from what we scientists call internal combustion.

So I explained that Albert inherits a certain amount, not too large, but still useful, of money under this will. 'How wonderful,' she said. 'Yes,' I told her, 'it would be a marvellous thing for him—only now the money goes to the Dogs' Home at Battersea.' I reached for my hat and started to walk to the door.

'One moment,' she cried. 'Why must my Albert lose this money, not to mention myself? I am getting ready a little exhibition of my paintings, which will cause a great furore if only they can be seen, but of course I need money to arrange the gallery.'

'I always thought the gallery paid you for pictures,' I said to her, because one should not lose an opportunity to learn a little about the technicalities of another kind of business.

'Formerly,' she explained to me, 'formerly, this did happen, but nowadays there are so many artists chasing so few galleries, the boot is on the other foot in a manner of speaking. But why does Albert's money go to a dogs' home?'

I could see she was very interested, so I explained that this eccentric uncle of Albert's doesn't like women, on the principle that all his life he can never leave women alone, and consequently has suffered a great deal. Therefore he wishes Albert not to get married, and (and I quoted from the will) in the event of Albert so doing, the money is going to the Battersea Dogs' Home, where only dogs will benefit from it; and this doesn't include any bitches at all, so against women is Albert's uncle.

I was about to leave when the girl said to me, 'Is there nothing can be done to break this inhuman will?'

I sighed and sat down to explain to her how sorry I am, but the damage is done; she is Albert's legal, married wife, signed, sealed and delivered, and that's all there is to it. It is too late to change the uncle's mind.

'One moment,' she said, 'I am not quite so signed, sealed and delivered as all that.'

'Madam,' I told her, 'I am not the kind of man to come between husband and wife. You are legal married, and that is good enough for me.' And I made to leave again.

'One moment,' she cried. 'This is a great sacrifice to me, but I will tell you the truth.' Good God, I said to myself, she is not going to tell me that Albert is illegal married twice, an illegal bigamist?

Then she explained how these two, young, romantic, go on a honeymoon down in the South, and they enjoy the honeymoon so much they decide to get married; and this arduous duty was performed for them by the parish priest down there. Naturally this information can only depress me, and I put my hat on again and told her good afternoon. It was finished, and I knew it. 'As I say,' I told her, game to the end, 'you are legal married, so the money goes to the dogs.'

'Not so fast,' she said, a calculating look on her face. 'In France, you must be married civically to be legal. This we didn't bother to do, so I am not, in law, Albert's wife, though it breaks my heart to tell you.'

Highly delighted, I struck a deal with her on the spot, paid her the cash after a little bargaining (and this girl, though an artist, was no piker when it came to making a bargain) and I got back as quickly as Moishe could drive me in his taxi to tell the children the glad tidings.

Then we celebrated the mysterious ways of destiny, though between ourselves I don't think it was destiny at all, just sheer artistic carelessness, and on principle I don't approve it. Nevertheless, I returned to London very satisfied with myself. A pity only we accountants do not have a trade newspaper in which I could announce how resourceful, nay, inspired, the firm of Botvinnik & Associates is in a crisis. Except, of course, it is not professional to advertise in my profession.

VII

BACK in the office everyone is running about like the fire is upstairs and not in Mendelman's factory at Watford. Mendelman's fire assessors, the insurance assessors, inspectors, policemen, the whole world is knocking at the door all day long. Mendelman has been telling everyone 'Botvinnik has the figures'—'Botvinnik knows everything'—'Ask Botvinnik'. Where is Mendelman all this time? The weather is very hot and he is sitting in a madeira chair with a glass of lemonade with ice in it, at Bournemouth at a very good hotel where every meal is a banquet. So I let the clerks in my office run about making up accounts and figures for the assessors, and the other assessors, and anybody else who wants figures.

The paper from yesterday is still lying on the doormat at my flat. The headline says FIRE AT WATFORD, then a little bit smaller, but still big enough, FACTORY DESTROYED, then underneath a little paragraph which says that a fine new light-engineering industry has been wiped out over night just at a time when we need all the industry we can get.

I phoned through to Mendelman at Bournemouth. After a lot of waiting and asking for Mr Mendelman to a girl, then to another girl, then to a man, then to another woman, Mendelman answers the phone.

'Well, Leo,' he asks, 'how is my beautiful Rosa?'

'Beautiful, Morris,' I tell him. 'She is very happy and is looking more lovely than ever.'

'Yes,' he says, 'she is a fine girl. Did you like Paris?'

'I liked Paris very much. Do you know the French for motor-car tyre? *Pneu*. You would never guess it in a thousand years.'

Morris laughed.

'It is a very funny language but pretty, and everybody talks it over there, so what can you do? Is everything arranged?'

'Morris,' I said, 'Morris, I have only just got back. I am not the prophet Elijah a fiery chariot is waiting to take me everywhere as quick as you can say Jackrobinson.'

'Well, of course, Leo,' he answers, 'naturally, of course. Don't worry, Leo, I know you will not waste time because you are an intelligent man and you know some things have not got long to wait.'

'How are you feeling, Morris?' I ask him.

'I am having a glass of cold lemonade under an umbrella on the veranda. It is very nice and hot here. But I am very upset.'

'Your heart?' I ask him.

'Yes,' he says, 'my heart gave a nasty jump when I heard my factory at Watford was burnt down. But what can I do? I am a sick man, Leo.'

'Just have a good rest, Morris,' I tell him, 'after all you are insured just in case this kind of thing should happen.'

'Of course,' he answers, 'but, Leo, a man builds a business, a new industry, and this happens. You think it is a judgement?'

'Who knows?' I answer.

'Well, anyway, you will see to everything?'

'Yes, Morris,' I say.

'Goodbye then, Leo. I am reading a good book. Bewick's *Birds*. The things birds can do. You would be surprised.'

'I am always having surprises even without birds,' I tell him.

To tell you the truth, although there was a great deal of excitement and running about, coming and going, telephone ringing, accounts, more accounts, it wasn't very different from usual. It was a bigger fire than we were used to, but what difference did that make to us? When you are an accountant it doesn't matter what the figures are so long as they balance. Botvinnik and Associates have always balanced, and why should they do any different this time? A man is a professional man first and foremost, then afterwards he is a father, a lover, a friend. For the time being I was only a professional man, an adding machine which drank lemon tea and could talk. I did my part, and in a few days it was all over and Mendelman's claim was going through. But although Mendelman was enjoying himself in Bournemouth, I still had my troubles.

I couldn't go and see Mendelman and tell him his libel plan was no good. How could I say to him, 'Morris, you have written your daughter is a whore, and believe me, you are right'? Because legally speaking what else was she but an adulteress, a harlot some lawyers would say, although, of course, she wasn't taking money, only for love. But love is something respectable people like to read about. When it happens they can become very nasty indeed. A love-child is just another bastard all of a sudden, and look at the fellow's poor legally married wife, and the girl took him away, and all this sort of thing. It is strange because romance must always lead to these other things. After all, love isn't just looking into a pair of eyes. But when it becomes serious so that you would expect people to say 'If they weren't really in love they wouldn't act like this,' what happens? Everyone is furious, and there is no end to it. In this life it is safer to make a mistake in your accounts than to fall in love. Love is very dangerous. It is the most dangerous thing in the world almost. Look at Napoleon with that Josephine. A lot of good she did him. And Caesar with Cleopatra. You would think a man with his experience would know better, but no. I seem to remember that she actually had a child by him; although, of course, in those days it was nothing even for a Queen.

But Mendelman, in spite of being philosophical about these things if they happened to other people, wouldn't be so pleased if he heard it was happening to his own beautiful daughter. He would drop stone dead, and that would do nobody any good. So, I had to think of something; me of all people. It shouldn't happen to a dog what was happening to me. And what is more, Mendelman so liked his libel idea that he would be very upset to give it up.

I have known him in the past do the same thing. There was the time when he bought all that shaving-cream from a company which went broke. He decided to put new labels on and sell it as hand-cream. He liked the idea so much, he insisted on doing it, although by the time he had taken the old labels off and printed new ones and put them on, the whole business showed a loss. He was Mendelman. He had to have a label in five colours.

I think he liked this idea in the same way. It was going to be difficult, but now I was so worried about Rosa I had to find a way. After all, it could have been my daughter who had got, God forbid, into trouble. I know it isn't a nice thing to say, and if anybody else said it I would be very angry. But couldn't it happen to anybody's daughter? Of course it could, and we might as well face the fact. And don't tell me you know a good man for abortions. How could you ask a girl like Rosa to do such a thing, kill a baby from a man she loved? It was a terrible situation but a way out had to be found. It wasn't the end of the world, a girl having a baby.

I thought for a long time, even while I spoke to other clients, even when I added up long columns of figures, how I should manage this business. What I decided to do may not have been very clever, but if Mendelman had told it to me I would have believed it, and better I couldn't do. I would tell Mendelman that Rosa being such a refined lady, due to her education, and moving in good-class circles on the Continent, she couldn't possibly have a libel like that against her. Her friends would never speak to her again. That was it, and even better. I would tell Mendelman that Rosa was friends with very fine important people and if the newspapers got hold of a story that she was being in a libel action, even if she won, even if it never went to the courts, they would think she wasn't good enough for them. Furthermore, and this was the fundamental part of my thesis, Rosa was engaged to a very nice boy of good family, and such a story would spoil everything, all her chances. She would lose the man she loved and become an old maid. And why? Because Mendelman was being so stubborn, he had to have a libel action with her. It was just conceit on his part. He wasn't thinking of Rosa at all. That poor girl, what a father to have! He would make a joke out of her, a terrible thing to do. Did he hate her? Didn't he care what happened to her life? It must all go for the sake of one of his crazy ideas? I was getting furious with Mendelman, when I remembered I wasn't talking to him. I was talking to myself in the office, and the chief clerk put his head round the door and said 'Did you call, Mr Botvinnik?' It was a wonderful idea.

When I left the office I was feeling happy. I had been in the jaws of calamity, but I had solved the whole problem. First the wife business and now the libel nonsense. Rosa would be all right. Mendelman would not drop dead. Everything was fine. It is the scientific training. It comes out with the right answer just when you have given the problem up. You can say what you like, but you can't beat a real scientific mind in a crisis. What is more, I even had an idea for providing for Rosa. After all, you must admit it would be terrible for Mendelman to go to the trouble of burning his factory down for the creditors.

VIII

MORRIS came back from Bournemouth looking brown and so well that for a moment I wondered whether it could be true that he was a man with death in his waistcoat pocket. His eyes were bright, and his face tanned and he wore a light tropical-weight grey suit very nicely cut, and a straw hat, like a tobacco-planter. He came into the office and waved his brown-paper cigarette at me.

'Did you enjoy yourself in Paris, Leo?' he said.

'I told you on the phone to Bournemouth,' I replied, 'It is very nice, but there is no place like home. Incidentally,' I added, laughing, 'do you know the French for motor-tyre?'

'You told me on the phone,' he said, 'how is Rosa?'

'Marvellous, I told you,' I said.

'She agrees to my plan? You must admit, Leo, it is a marvellous plan.'

'No,' I said.

'What do you mean *No*?' he said. 'No what, no who, Rosa says no, you say no?' He got excited very quickly, that Mendelman.

I explained to him very tactfully that Rosa was engaged to

a promising composer, and everything would be ruined if we went ahead with his plan.

'And to tell you the truth, Morris,' I added, 'I for one am not sorry, because I think it was a very brilliant but if I may say so, a slightly mad idea. Also these great ideas sometimes backfire.'

He was quiet for a moment. His lips moved two or three times, little movements which didn't mean very much. He finished his cigarette and stubbed it out.

'All right,' he said, 'what shall we do instead?' and I could see that if someone was to come into the office now and put his own crazy idea up to Mendelman he would have laughed his head off. 'I never heard such a stupid idea' he would say. He had dropped it, and already it seemed to him impossible that such a scheme should ever have been suggested. That was the kind of salesman he was.

Then I put to him my own suggestion, a simple professional plan, not brilliant, not flashy, not poetic, but it would do the job he wanted done.

My proposal was simply this. That Rosa should become a partner in Botvinnik & Associates. We would make up a partnership agreement, and Mendelman would pay me say five thousand pounds in return for Rosa's interest in my firm, and we would guarantee to Rosa an income of five hundred pounds a year. How we would get the five thousand was more difficult. We could pre-date the agreement and try to make Mendelman's debt to my firm a first charge upon his business. We could even have Rosa Products issue Botvinnik & Associates with a debenture to that amount so that it became a first charge on the firm. Then when the insurance claim was paid, Botvinnik would have to be paid out before anyone else.

'Why not make it for ten thousand, Leo?' Mendelman asked.

'Why not aim high and pay Rosa seven hundred and fifty a year?'

'Because my dear Morris,' I said, 'we are not doing a deal together for a hundred gross trousers. My business is not worth ten thousand, but a half-share in it could be worth five thousand, and we must be practical about this and stick to the facts.'

I think Mendelman was more relieved at my suggestion than he seemed. He accepted all my points. A man comes to an end with everything. Everything has its end. A gambler can get tired of cards, so tired that ace, king, queen, jack in a hand means nothing to him. A glutton sooner or later will sicken at the thought of food. A woman can have too many diamonds. A Don Juan too many women. The more flesh, the more worms, as Mendelman used to say, Mendelman, a business man who had lived through enough businesses. He was tired of arguing and scheming. He was glad for me to take over the problem.

'So you will look after Rosa,' he said.

'Yes,' I told him, 'I will be very pleased to do so, but apart from all that, you are after all buying a piece of my business for her.'

'That is so,' he said, 'it is all being done on a business-like basis. Business, after all, is business.'

'Absolutely,' I agreed, 'also what have I to work for anyway —this way Rosa will benefit from my meaningless life.'

'This is what makes life something,' he said. 'Well, and what about my fire? Does it go through all right?'

'It appears to be going through very satisfactory,' I said. 'How did it happen?'

Mendelman laughed, sat back in the chair, lit another cigarette, and told me.

'You shouldn't smoke so much in your condition,' I said.

'You are wrong, Leo,' he said, 'it is in exactly my condition that it doesn't matter. I could smoke all day and all night, through my ears as well as my mouth, and it wouldn't make much difference. But who wants to smoke as much as that? Anyhow, let me get on with the story.'

Mendelman was always a good judge of human nature, and when it came to burning down his factory this power of judgement served him very well. Everything depended on his night-watchman, because, after all, if the night-watchman was actually watching at night no harm could come to the factory even from its owner. This problem Mendelman had carefully considered.

He had always taken a great interest in his employees. He was godfather to seventeen children and always gave good christening, wedding and Christmas presents. Some thought that Mendelman interfered too much in the affairs of his employees, and the night-watchman himself was just such a case. He had been employed for over two years about the factory as an odd-job man, and very efficient and reliable he was, although well past retiring age. Mendelman used to talk to him for a half-hour whenever he visited the factory. Philosophy and religion they used to discuss together, and being as the night-watchman was a Scottish Presbyterian, they got on very well together, almost always agreeing. Sometimes they disagreed, and then the Scotsman would threaten to leave. But Mendelman used to beg him to stay, and perhaps give him a small rise as a proof of his good faith. 'Fergus,' he told me often, 'is a good clear thinker. His ideas on making a republic out of Scotland are completely sound. What is more, if Scotland was a separate country it would have many business advantages.' Mendelman would always continue, 'Fergus has only one fault.

He can't leave the girls alone. If a girl should come past him, straightaway he is an octopus with sixty-three hands. All after the girl. It causes bad feeling.'

What caused especially bad feeling was that for some reason girls liked Fergus with his hands. He was an old man, and yet from what Mendelman told me, I think some of those girls went out of their way to turn their bottoms in his direction, if you will excuse the expression.

'What?' I said to Mendelman, 'such an old man to still be after the girls?'

'Leo,' he answered me, 'with some old men things are even worse than with boys.'

Anyhow, through this Fergus the factory was burnt down, and this was just an example of Mendelman's great luck, for it was certainly through no interference on his part that the fat girl got pregnant.

This fat girl, you might say, was sure to get pregnant in the end. A girl who spends so many dinner hours in the disused shed on the other side of the lot should expect that. But it must have been a great surprise to her when Fergus put the finish to her nonsense. When Mendelman heard about it he didn't bat an eyelid. 'All right,' he said, 'let Fergus marry the fat girl. Sometimes it happens this way round.' That's how broadminded he was with other people. But Fergus didn't want to get married. The fat girl cried and cried, until Mendelman was absolutely sick and tired of the whole business. 'Look Fergus,' he shouted, 'I am absolutely sick and tired of this whole business. Either you marry the fat girl, or by my life, you can go.'

'Good afternoon, Mr Mendelman,' said the Scotsman.

'Just a minute, Fergus,' Morris called after him. 'Don't be so hasty.'

'Pardon me, Mr Mendelman,' Fergus replied, 'you cannot

talk such words to a free-born Scot, so with your leave, I'll be off.' Eventually Fergus agreed to stay. But only if he got a change of job. He agreed to marry the fat girl, but only if he got the night-watchman's house. He got them, and was married. From which it follows, that on the night on which Mendelman called at his factory intending to burn it down, the night-watchman was not there. Where was he? Where do you think? He was in bed with the fat girl.

Now Mendelman's factory before he took it over was the Bigga Balloon Co., specializing in all types of rubber goods. Taken over with some warehouse equipment were several boxes of balloons and suchlike. What with these and the night-watchman it was certain that the factory should burn. But you have to admire the artistry with which Mendelman managed it.

Other men might have been satisfied to soak some old rags in petrol, set fire to them, and trust in God. Not Mendelman. He carefully installs paraffin central heating radiators a couple of weeks before. Then when he passes by the factory late that night, he takes a can of paraffin out of the storehouse, and a dozen balloons from a tea-chest. These he fills with paraffin. He ties them together with thread soaked in paraffin. Then he sets light to the thread and leaves.

He heard five or six muffled pops as the balloons touched off. 'I didn't know it would work,' he said, 'so you can imagine how happy I was when I heard them. Pop, pop, pop.'

'Pop, pop,' I said. 'What terrible risks you take, Morris.'

'I must admit,' he answered, 'perhaps I am a little bit of a fire-raiser, because I enjoyed it.' What can you do with such a man?

'But I went to all that trouble for nothing,' Morris concluded. 'Now Rosa will be looked after by your firm, and——'

'Please, Morris,' I said, 'if you don't like my ideas get on with your own, but please don't expect me to take any more interest in the entire affair.'

'Don't get so blown up, Leo,' he said, 'keep your sense of proportion. I realize you have done the best you can.' I would have been rude to him, except that he went on without a pause, 'Now we must plan an extra-special wedding for Rosa and her boy. When are they to arrive? We will invite five hundred couples and eat caviare out of ladles.'

'I think they would prefer a quiet little wedding, Morris,' I said.

'Do you think five hundred couples is enough?' he answered. In a matter of ten seconds I was helping plan a tremendous wedding. Oy.

IX

I AM sorry to say that this wedding never took place. In another way I am not sorry, because although the plans (it was to be a proper occasion) were all fixed, Mendelman had not taken into consideration one small fact. It is a beautiful thing to see the confidence a father can have in his daughter. Mendelman arranged for the ceremony and everything, and not once did it occur to him that there might be, let us say, a technical objection. For my part, I kept trying to think of diplomatic ways to tell him, but who can be diplomatic about such a thing? Albert was a lovely boy, but he just happened by some ridiculous oversight, to be a Catholic.

When Rosa and Albert came back from Paris, Mendelman arranged a quiet dinner for the four of us, and you could see that he really had taken a fancy to Albert as a son-in-law. After the dinner, Mendelman insisted on the young couple going to an opera he had bought them tickets for, because he thought it was the right thing to do on such an occasion. After they left, he explained to me that he liked the boy so much he didn't want to have him around too long in case he started to discover his faults.

'Now, Leo,' he said, 'we can sit here and drink brandy and smoke cigars——'

'You smoke too many cigars,' I told him.

'——And talk about old times, Ah, Leo,' he said, 'it's a marvellous thing to see your family provided for. They should be very happy, those two. At least, what I mean to say is that when they fight, they should enjoy making it up afterwards, which is the true test of marriage.'

Mendelman took his brandy-glass and warmed it gently with his hands as he left the table and made himself comfortable in a deep leather chair by the fire. I sat in a smaller chair opposite. 'Well,' Mendelman sighed, 'it has been not such a bad life. It's a pity you didn't see that fire, Leo. It really was something. You would have enjoyed it. I am going to tell you now,' he continued, 'the truth about life. This is the truth——'

Then the telephone rang, and I went to answer it.

It was my chief clerk. All the evening, he had been trying to find me, he said. The inspectors for the insurance company were not satisfied with Mendelman's claim. 'They sounded a little upset, Mr Botvinnik,' he said.

'You should send them from me, Harris, in the morning,' I I told him, 'a big bunch of flowers.' Then I went back to Mendelman.

It is a pity the phone didn't ring a little later, because then Mendelman would have told me the truth about life. As it was, I had to work it out for myself. Mendelman, with the bowl of

C

brandy cooling in his hands, and a smile on his face, my mad friend Morris Mendelman was dead.

I removed the cigar, which had fallen onto his jacket where it had already burnt a small, perfectly round hole.

'Mendelman,' I said to him, the tears slowly running down my cheeks, 'the truth about life is——' But like Mendelman, I forgot the point. So I just cried for a while instead.

I I

A Village like Yours

THE FINEST PIPE-MAKER IN RUSSIA

MY GREAT-GRANDFATHER was certainly the finest pipe-maker in Russia—or at least in that part where he lived. Not only did everyone worth noticing buy a pipe from my great-grandfather, but even landowners and the owner of the large timber business in the next village came to him for their best pipes even if they sometimes smoked others made by inferior craftsmen. And so my great-grandfather was a very famous man indeed, for, although you can live your whole life and only hear of Napoleon when someone digs up a French coin or an old rusted sabre, you cannot smoke a good pipe without remembering who made it, and you wish him many more years, so that he can go on making you pipes, although, of course, my great-grandfather's pipes were not such bad workmanship that you needed perhaps more than two in a life-time. But you would be pleased for him to live a long time, anyway. Once, however, my great-grandfather made a bad pipe—and even then he made it bad for a good reason. He was the finest pipe-maker in Russia and would never have made a bad pipe without having a very good reason.

It happens that this pipe was bad because of what took place on a Sabbath morning. Not that my great-grandfather made the pipe on a Sabbath I would not like anyone to think that of him. Any pipe made on a Sabbath morning—it goes without saying—is not likely to draw well after the Sabbath has gone out. And my great-grandfather was not the man to make pipes at any time except when a respectable man should make pipes. No, my great-grandfather was not in his workshop on this par-ticular Sabbath morning. He was in the synagogue with the

other men of the village. Where else would he be? But it had
to be on this particular morning that somebody should want to
make himself a nuisance by coming to my great-grandfather for
a pipe. My young grandfather was not at the synagogue. If he
had been thirteen yet and confirmed, he would have been there.
As it was, he was sitting in my great-grandfather's workshop
playing with a chisel and a piece of wood. Suddenly my great-
grandmother rushed into the workshop, calling out: 'So where
are you, Yankele? Why don't you answer? Put down your
father's tools. What do you mean on a Sabbath morning playing with tools? Run quickly to the synagogue and tell your
father he should come home straightaway.'

My grandfather was young, but he was not so young that he
did not know my great-grandfather to have a big, heavy hand
all hard with working wood. So he did not rush out like a mad
person straightaway to do as my great-grandmother had asked.
Instead, he thought for a moment, and then he said: 'Supposing I go and tell my father he should come home. What will he
say? He won't say anything. He will give me a clout on the
head. On the Sabbath he doesn't want to know about the
house. Only if it's burning down should you try to fetch him
from the synagogue.' Which was true, because my great-
grandfather was a pious man. He used to say: 'If God has
given us six days, can't we spare him one?' And who could
answer him? There was no answer. Everyone stood dumb.

But my great-grandmother said: 'Yankele, if you don't hurry
to the synagogue and bring home your father I will give you
such a clout on the head you won't argue any more.'

This made my young grandfather think: If I stay here, I get
a clout on the head. If I go to the synagogue, I get a clout on
the head. At least let me get away from the nearest one first.
But he looked obedient and said to my great-grandmother: 'All

right, but what shall I tell my father so that he won't give me a clout on the head? Why should he come home right away? The house isn't burning.'

My great-grandmother could see that what my grandfather said was reasonable, so she answered quickly: 'Outside is waiting a lord with a big carriage with horses and a coachman, and he wants father to make him an extra-special pipe.'

Not many lords came to my great-grandfather's workshop. 'If they are satisfied with inferior workmanship, it is their own business,' my great-grandfather used to say. So that when a lord came my great-grandfather was bound to be very excited. My young grandfather was also excited, and rushed out to see the carriage and the horses and, of course, the lord himself.

The lord was in the kitchen sitting by the stove. He was a big man, with a lot of furs on him, and he was sucking a thick cheroot. My young grandfather could see he needed a pipe badly and told him: 'I am going to fetch my father, who is the finest pipe-maker in Russia, to make you a pipe.'

And the big man said, 'Good. Here is a sixpence for you. Run quickly.' And to my great-grandmother he said, 'Have you any vodka in the house?'

My grandfather ran out of the house without even putting his hat on. It was snow everywhere, you understand—real heavy thick snow covering everything, not like in this country, where an inch is a lot, but real heavy thick snow. When it melted, sometimes you could find a cow which had been lost all the winter, or sometimes even a drunken man last heard of months ago. But my young grandfather was very strong although he was not yet confirmed, and he was thinking of the boiled butter-beans he could buy at school with the sixpence, so he ran over the snow like a wolf, and the cold did not bother him.

Still, the synagogue was two miles away, and before my grandfather got here he stopped running, and when he stopped running he began to think of how (without letting himself in for a clout on the head) he could ask my great-grandfather to leave the synagogue. When he got there he still had not thought of a way, so he went up to my great-grandfather, who was praying with a big shawl round him, and he touched his hand and waited. Then my great-grandfather, who was a very big man indeed, looked down and smiled through his beard and nodded his head and went on praying. He thought my young grandfather had come to the synagogue to be with the men praying, and said to himself, 'Perhaps he will be a student and a teacher after all. Perhaps he will turn out to be a credit, although he is developing late.'

But my young grandfather was feeling very nervous with his hand in his pocket fingering the sixpence which the lord had given him, because he suddenly remembered that he would get a clout on the head even if it was only because he had taken money on the Sabbath. After a while he looked up at my great-grandfather again and said quietly: 'My mother wants you to come home.'

My great-grandfather was very surprised, and replied: 'What?'

My young grandfather looked away and said even more quietly: 'She wants you to come home because someone wishes to see you.'

My great-grandfather looked even more surprised and was also beginning to look angry. He blew through his beard: 'What? Yankele, on a Sabbath morning you come to synagogue to bring me home to the house? What does it mean? I will give you a clout on the head.'

My young grandfather knew to expect this, so he had already

moved a few yards away, and he answered: 'A lord is waiting by the house. He wants you to make him a pipe. He is a lord with a carriage and horses and even a coachman. And he is wearing a big fur coat.'

But my great-grandfather still looked angry and surprised. It had never happened before, this being sent messages at the synagogue in the middle of the Sabbath morning to come home and make a pipe. Well, what could you expect from a woman and a boy not yet confirmed: but this was too much already. He chewed his beard and said: 'A lord is waiting? Well, and why shouldn't he wait? Tell this lord he must wait for my lord. And leave me alone on a Sabbath morning, Yankele, or I'm telling you I will give you such a clout on the head you will never forget it.'

My grandfather was already out of the synagogue. He ran for a time, but because it was two miles back to the house he began to walk and think of how he could tell the lord what my great-grandfather's message was without getting maybe the hardest clout of all.

He saw the lord walking up and down outside the house, and he was breathing out big clouds of steam like the horses, which were also breathing out big clouds, but the lord's clouds were even bigger than the horses'. The lord was walking up and down with his hands in fur gloves behind his back, so my grandfather went first to the closet which was at the bottom of the piece of ground on which my great-grandfather kept my great-grandmother's cow, Masha, and his own cherry trees. He hid his sixpence under the seat, and then called out to the lord what the message was and quickly ran back to the closet. My grandfather heard the lord shout at my great-grandmother: 'Well, then, must I wait a month for this pipe-maker? Is he a lord, or am I? Must I wait until the thaw? Well, must I wait all day?' And the lord got into his carriage and his horses pulled him away to the inn at the next village, which was on the other side of the hill.

When my great-grandfather arrived back from the synagogue he greeted my great-grandmother, and the next thing he said was: 'Now, Yetta, is dinner ready yet?' And then he asked: 'Where is that Yankele? And what did he want? And don't you know any better than to send him for me on a Sabbath morning? What do you mean?' When my great-grandmother explained to him he said: 'Aha! So the lord is getting tired of his bad pipes. When he tries everybody else's pipes and finds out how bad they are, he comes to me. Aha!'

Then in the afternoon, when my grandfather had come out of the closet, he was taken with my great-grandfather to the next village, to the inn. The inn smelt very strong. 'Faugh, faugh,' said my great-grandfather.

All the peasants who spotted my great-grandfather greeted him with respect, because they knew he was the finest pipe-maker in Russia and a credit to the neighbourhood, and besides that, he was a very big man, who had beaten a drunken peasant once who shouted after him in the street.

The lord was drinking in the inn, and when he saw my great-grandfather he shouted: 'Well, are you the pipe-maker? Why do you keep me waiting? Are you a bigger lord that you can keep me waiting?'

My great-grandfather answered him: 'Sir, if when you are in the army your general calls for you, you go?'

The lord drank a glassful of vodka and replied: 'Yes, of course you go. In the army when a general calls you, you go.'

My great-grandfather continued: 'And how long do you stay with your general?'

The lord looked at my great-grandfather with an unpleasant

look: 'So you have not done any military service? What do you mean, how long? When a general calls you, you don't ask how long. You stay there until he tells you to go away.'

My great-grandfather paused. All the peasants were standing around looking at him as if they were dumb, and my young grandfather knew that they thought he was a clever man because he was getting the lord into such a deep argument. My grandfather had heard the argument before and this time he did not think it so clever. Why argue with a lord? With a peasant, yes; with my great-grandmother, yes; with the rabbi even, yes; but with a lord—it was like arguing with a policeman. But my great-grandfather was completing the argument: 'I was called by my general,' he said, pulling his whiskers, 'and I had to stay until he told me to go.'

All the peasants looked at one another, and the lord drank another glass of vodka, and my grandfather thought: it is a very fine thing to make arguments, but with a lord I don't think it is so clever.

Then the lord drank still another glass of vodka, whereupon he shouted: 'All right then, all right. Well, then, I want a pipe, a specially good pipe for a present for a prince. You hear, a present for a prince. It must be a good pipe, the best.'

My great-grandfather looked down his nose, and he made some more argument: 'My pipes are all the best. Would you be coming to me for a pipe if it wasn't the best?'

And my grandfather thought: arguments, always arguments he's making.

The lord went on: 'Very well. This one must be better. And, most important of all, it must have a carved eagle on the bowl. It is no good without a carved eagle. It is for a prince, and he must have an eagle, otherwise it is no good.'

My grandfather expected more arguments, but, instead, my

great-grandfather said very quietly: 'Very well. With a carved
eagle it will be good, otherwise it is no good. Right.'

'Yes,' said the lord. 'It must have an eagle, and I want it
tomorrow.'

Now my grandfather really expected arguments. Sabbath
was not yet out, and the lord wanted his pipe tomorrow! When
could it be made? To make a good pipe takes a long time. My
great-grandfather liked to make a pipe in his own time. You
said to him one day: 'Moishe, you know I would like a pipe.'
And he would say: 'Yes, a good pipe is a very good thing.' And
two or three months later when he met you in the street he
would say: 'Here you are. Here is a pipe you will like.'

But for this lord a pipe had to be made with an eagle, otherwise it was no good. 'All right,' said my great-grandfather. And
he sat up all night to make a pipe with an eagle carved on the
bowl.

When in the morning my grandfather went into the workshop, he saw the pipe lying on the bench. It had a fine eagle
carved on it, with big wings curling down to the stem, and the
wings were made up of Hebrew letters carefully carved to look
like a row of feathers.

The lord came early with his coach and horses, and he came
in and saw the pipe and paid my great-grandfather what he
asked—twelve roubles—and he liked the finely carved eagle
very much. He gave my grandfather another sixpence, and now
my grandfather was fingering two sixpences in his pocket.

Afterwards my great-grandfather said to my grandfather:
'This lord must have an eagle carved, but the pipe is not so
important. He knows what one of his generals can do, but my
general is not so important. All right, then, I have given him a
pipe I should wish my worst friend. Two, three years a pipe like
this could last'—my great-grandfather knew when he made a

bad pipe because he was certainly the finest pipe-maker in Russia—'and I have carved on it the Prayer for the Dead. How long can a prince like that live, anyway?'

But my grandfather thought: for two sixpences I can have boiled butter-beans every day for a year.

THE LAW-BREAKER

AT THE school to which my grandfather went there was no privy. At least there was a privy but it was attached to the synagogue which the village millionaire had given to the community, and it was always kept locked except on Saturday when of course it was required. But at the back of the schoolroom there was a big piece of ground, and when a boy raised his hand in the middle of a difficult text the teacher used to say: 'All right, then, all right, go into the yard. I am waiting.'

The teacher, who was called Yaacov, was a short fat man with a black dusty beard which was going grey perhaps though you couldn't see that because of the dust. He could only read a book by holding it up close to his face, but he never needed to look closely to see if my grandfather was reading wrong, because Yaacov knew everything by heart, and anyhow my grandfather normally did read wrong. On a Friday, Yaacov went round to all the fathers of the boys he taught to collect his teaching-money. He used to make it a little more or less according to who he was collecting from, and when he was teaching a boy for confirmation he added a little for the extra strain on his voice and for writing the special confirmation discourse which was spoken by each boy. It was worth the extra, too, because Yaacov was a clever scholar and every confirmation speech was a little different, although there were the usual thanks in it to the boy's mother and father and to Yaacov as well, who was always called in these speeches 'my learned and respected teacher, the scholar Yaacov ben Yitschok'.

When Yaacov himself went outside to the yard he left his

oldest son (the one with pimples and long side curls) in charge. This son was his cleverest and, though very ugly, was regarded as a good prospective match being as he was so clever and had such a good business head. When his father went out he would unfold a paper which came to him from Moscow every week, lay it on the table in front of the class and offer the older boys a read of a column for a farthing. It was no good expecting to read more than one column for a farthing because he covered up the part of the paper for which you hadn't contracted, and if your eyes moved over to it he shouted out, 'Breach of contract—another farthing.' Usually he sold at least three or four columns to different boys while his father was outside, and in this way made quite a nice profit on his papers, as well as out of the butter-beans which he boiled at home and brought to the school to sell to the boys.

Why his father was always so long outside didn't bother him. The longer Yaacov was away the better it was for the newspaper business. All the other boys too didn't mind how long Yaacov was out in the yard. They read the paper, held fighting competitions, and ate the butter-beans which they had been sitting on all through the lessons. As they used to wrap the beans in their handkerchiefs before sitting on them it was quite all right. My grandfather got a clean handkerchief every Saturday morning.

Now often my grandfather watched Yaacov in the yard standing in one corner for a few minutes then moving lower down the fence and standing there for a few minutes, then moving lower down still and yet again standing there for a few minutes, then at last moving across the yard to another corner. He thought that this was a very unusual and impressive business and sometimes back at home he would pretend he was Yaacov in the yard and shuffle from one corner to another muttering to himself. Soon he became very good at being Yaacov, and one day at school he took some friends into the yard and without warning began to shuffle from one side to the other muttering all the time.

All the boys laughed very much and kept on asking him to do it again. They said he was certain to become a teacher because he was so good at being Yaacov, but he said no, he would sooner be a soldier even than a school teacher, a sentiment with which most of them agreed. After this it became his favourite way to make the boys laugh at school when Yaacov wasn't looking. Once when the clever son was busy arguing with an older boy about whether he had been reading too much of the paper or not, my grandfather with great daring followed Yaacov quietly out into the yard. Five other little boys followed my grandfather. As Yaacov shuffled from one place to another my grandfather shuffled after him and after my grandfather shuffled the five little boys and then they quietly returned to the classroom. They found this so funny that afterwards whenever Yaacov went out back, grunting to his son to meanwhile look after the class, they followed him out and shuffled after him, and Yaacov never knew because he always concentrated so on his work. The boys even looked forward to school, until at last as they trooped out after Yaacov, Yaacov's son saw them and shouted to his father, and Yaacov turned and saw them for the first time, and chased them in, but he only caught my grandfather who was the smallest. Then he made my grandfather read a very difficult place in the Pentateuch, getting him to explain the part where it says: 'Thou shalt not baste the kid in the milk of its mother.'

Now my grandfather knew that this had something to do with eating or not eating but he couldn't remember which. After sitting there with Yaacov breathing down on his face for some minutes saying: 'Well, then? What, what? Come on, then, you learned one, tell me,' he admitted that he did as a matter of fact find it a bit difficult to recollect. Then Yaacov shouted, 'Oho! To mock his teacher is not hard for him, but to learn is too much!' And he gave my grandfather a very hard knock with a book on the back of his head and told him to get outside and go home to tell his father why his learned and respected teacher refused to have him in the class.

My grandfather ran out of the class crying, which was the only sound heard for some while, because Yaacov stood in front glaring at them all, and no one dared to say a word or whistle or make even the slightest noise by breathing too hard.

My grandfather stopped crying quickly after he left. Even more quickly he decided he certainly wouldn't go home to catch trouble from my great-grandfather, who being a pious man would certainly be very annoyed with my grandfather for making a nuisance of himself to the teacher. So my grandfather sat down in a ditch by the side of the road—as it was summer it was very dry and warm—to think over the whole business. While he was thinking he found a spider running from under a stone so he caught it and kept it in his hand till he made a small hole surrounded with stones. Then he put the spider into the hole and pushed it about with a piece of straw, making it go in different directions.

All the time he was doing this he thought about how Yaacov had hit him, and for no reason at all. Did all the boys laugh or did they not? Everyone laughed, he was a public entertainer, and yet Yaacov hit him. Anyhow, there had been others following Yaacov all over the yard, so why should my grandfather get the blame? And as for my great-grandfather, he always sided with the teacher. He believed anyone who said my grandfather had stolen some Hungarian plums or had knocked off somebody's high hat, which he had, but still. My great-grandfather said my grandfather was only good for a soldier, and that if the Army came to collect him they would only get thanks and a couple of roubles from my great-grandfather.

Everything he did was wrong. No one cared about him except to give him a knock on the head or to shout at him. And how should he know why a kid should never be basted in the milk of its mother? Who wanted to baste kids anyhow? If he was a soldier he would show that Yaacov. Throw his skull-cap into some mud, and then put dead rats in his house. And he would carry money on Saturdays, swear in Russian, and get drunk like Bonifas the Cobbler. He would even eat meat and drink some milk with it!

When my grandfather suddenly thought of that he stopped pushing the spider about. He thought of it again, wrinkling his mouth as if tasting the two foods together. Or what about some roast liver with butter—why not eat them together? He swallowed hard, sat up in the ditch and made a decision. If everyone said he was a no-good, very well then, he would show them they were right. And my grandfather jumped up out of the ditch and ran home.

When he got to my great-grandfather's house he stopped at the gate. Then he went round the back, tip-toed through the yard so that no one could hear him, and before going in, looked through the kitchen window to see if my great-grandmother was cooking. The kitchen was empty, so he walked quietly in and opened the cupboard where food was kept. On one shelf were all the milk foods, buttermilk and milk from my great-grandmother's cow (which was called Masha) and cheese and butter. My grandfather put his finger into the butter and brought out some of it. Then he put most of it back because he thought that, after all, he only needed to eat a little of it with liver. Then he looked over the other shelf where there was cold roast meat, some boiled fish, and some pieces of chicken liver which my great-grandmother was keeping for her husband's supper. He took a small piece of liver, looked round quickly, and ran out of the house.

My grandfather ran right away from the house, up a hill where there were still trenches from where soldiers had come past a long time ago before even my great-grandfather was a boy, leaving behind them only a few coins and sometimes a bone and of course the trenches.

When he got to the top of the hill he sat down again to think, but first putting the small piece of butter on to one bundle of grass and the piece of liver on to another. He thought of everything everyone would say when they heard what he had done. Then his hair stood on end as he suddenly remembered a fact. All the boys, even some of the older ones who had been confirmed, always said that if anyone ever ate milk with meat something terrible would happen, not only to that person but to the whole village a calamity would happen. My grandfather looked down from the hill-top. In the village lights were already on in some of the houses. He saw a light go on in the baker's house just behind his shop where you could get fresh white rolls, and in his mind's mouth he tasted the crisp bread. He watched a light go on in his uncle Yossef's house and remembered that his uncle Yossef always gave him some money every Chanuka. But he thought again of my great-grandfather and of Yaacov, and feeling very angry he quickly put the butter with the liver together into his mouth, and swallowed them, thinking: serve them right.

Even as he felt the mixed taste go from his tongue he felt sorry. He was sorry because he was already beginning to feel slightly sick, but also because when he looked down towards the village he knew that something terrible was certain to happen to everyone there because of his sin which he had just sinned. Yet more than anything else he was sorry because he remembered Yaacob saying that anyone who ate meat with butter was certain to die young. And wasn't my grandfather young? The more he thought about it the less pleased with himself did he feel. Groaning quietly but proud that at least he was the only boy in the village to die in this particular way, he lay back in the trench and waited.

It grew darker and darker. All the time the dew fell heavier until all the grass around my grandfather became soaked. There was some long grass over his face and some drops of dew fell off from the top of the blades of grass suddenly, and ran down the side of his nose and he jumped up thinking his last moment had certainly come. But it hadn't, so he sat down again leaning his head against the side of the trench, thinking how sorry my great-grandmother would be, even if he had sinfully eaten liver with butter.

Then my grandfather fell asleep but he didn't sleep for very long. In less than half an hour he woke up because it had grown very cold and he wasn't wearing his overcoat. As soon as he woke up he felt hungry, and as soon as he felt hungry he remembered he was dead and couldn't eat. So he got out of the trench and saw that the village was still there and realized that he was a demon or something. Then he felt his face and found that although it was wet with dew it still felt like his old face, and on top of everything else he really was very hungry. He thought the whole thing out. If he was dead, could he be hungry and yet not eat? Was it a punishment? On the other hand maybe God hadn't seen him do the sin? Perhaps God didn't care? Maybe God was too busy to watch my grandfather the whole time to make sure he didn't eat liver with butter? In which case my grandfather could get away with all kinds of little sins. He might carry a mouse to synagogue in his pocket on Saturday. My grandfather felt suddenly very strong. He stood up to the top of his height, very straight. Then he ran down the hill, very pleased with himself.

When my grandfather got back to the house, my great-grandfather looked up and saw there was something different from usual in the face of his son. He had never seen my grandfather look so pleased after coming back from school. Neither had he ever known him home so late. Usually he was home too early, running back as soon as he could get out, never wanting to stay and listen to the older boys discuss reverent problems. So my great-grandfather smiled at him and said:

'You are late, my son. Have you been learning for so long in the school?'

My grandfather, still looking very pleased, thought he'd try a little lie and said that he had. My great-grandfather wondered if perhaps he had been wrong about his son, that the goodness and the intentions of God were impossible for any man to be assured of, and he asked my grandfather what he had been learning. The only thing my grandfather could now remember was the piece from the Pentateuch about basting a kid in the milk of its mother. This he expounded to my great-grandfather, explaining that it meant that no one should eat liver with butter, and that if they did they would certainly die young.

My great-grandfather was so pleased at my grandfather's knowledge, he offered him some of the chicken liver my great-grandmother had prepared for him alone. But my grandfather said no, he couldn't eat the father's own food like that, he would rather take some fish. And my great-grandfather thought this was certainly a miracle and that Yaacov was indeed a great scholar, and my grandfather would surely grow up to be a pious man and a teacher. My grandfather was thinking for his part, that he would be terribly sick if he ever ate liver again, even without butter.

THE DAY AUNT CHAYA WAS BURIED

ONE Sabbath my great-grandfather was singing some verses of the service which belonged to the cantor. The cantor sang loud. My great-grandfather, who had a very strong voice, sang louder still so that one or two men in the synagogue felt uncomfortable and wished that Reb Sholem Pinsk the beadle would arrive and quietly request my great-grandfather to let the cantor earn the few pennies he was paid.

But where was Reb Sholem? This was really a question to ask, for where should a beadle be on Sabbath morning if not in synagogue. Then, suddenly, like an explosion, in ran Reb Sholem waving his spectacles in one hand and his praying-shawl in the other. He rushed up to my great-grandfather (who was singing even louder) and pulled at his coat. 'Why shouldn't I sing?' asked my great-grandfather. 'What sort of a cantor does he think he is anyway? My own cow can sing better.' Reb Sholem pulled his arm. 'Listen,' he wheezed between coughing and spitting for he was an old man to have been running so fast. 'Listen,' he grunted, 'the bronze horse at Nevel has been blown up.' 'What?' cried all the men around, 'The bronze horse at Nevel? You don't say so?' they said.

'I'm telling you,' shouted Reb Sholem Pinsk, 'The bronze horse standing in the market-place at Nevel has been blown up.'

The cantor was taking advantage of the disturbance to get through a few verses without assistance. But what was the use since everyone was listening to Reb Sholem. The cantor stopped singing and called out in his rich voice, 'Reb Sholem, why should we care whether the bronze horse at Nevel is blown up or not? This is the Sabbath and we are at worship. What do we care about the bronze horse at Nevel?'

'He's right,' said my great-grandfather. 'He can't sing but what he says is true. What do I care about the bronze horse at Nevel. I already have enough worries of my own,' and he began to sing again where he had left off before.

'He's right,' said all the men. '*We* should worry about the bronze horse at Nevel,' and they straightened their praying-shawls and went back to their seats.

Reb Sholem pulled at my great-grandfather's coat again even harder. 'Believe me,' he said, 'you should be worried. We should all be worried.'

'You should have no false gods, even a bronze horse, Reb Sholem, especially as you are, late on shabbos or not, the beadle,' called the cantor severely.

'God forbid,' answered Reb Sholem, 'let all bronze idols be blown up. But—' and again he pulled at my great-grandfather's coat, 'not by your youngest sister Chaya.'

'What?' shouted my great-grandfather. 'At least he has stopped singing,' thought the cantor.

'Your youngest sister Chaya has blown up the bronze horse at Nevel,' repeated Reb Sholem. 'God help us,' whispered my great-grandfather and walked straight out of the synagogue. 'Now perhaps I can sing without an ass braying' thought the cantor.

When my great-grandfather arrived home he was greeted by the sound of crying and voices all asking different questions at the same time. The family was gathered around Aunt Chaya asking her questions, and weeping for her, and so worrying the poor woman that, true as she remained in principle to the Revolution, she was beginning to wish she had never learnt how to make bombs, nor how to throw them, particularly in the direction of, for example, bronze horses. But everyone was silenced by my great-grandfather shouting, 'Hold your tongues, you geese, or I will give you something to cry about. You understand me?' Then he continued politely, 'First you must understand, my dear Chaya, that we are very pleased to see you.' Everyone shouted out, 'Certainly', 'I should think so', 'Naturally'.

'Be quiet,' my great-grandfather shouted. He turned again to his young sister. 'Chaya,' he said in a solemn voice, 'Chaya, I have always said to you, make your own decisions and go your own way, for if you must associate with riff-raff then it must surely be God's intention and it is not for me to interfere. But now you have done some terrible thing and although God certainly knows what you have done and why you have done it, I do not, and if it is not troubling you too much I should like to hear the entire story.' And my great-grandfather sat down in his chair, in which, of course, no one else was sitting.

Aunt Chaya was a little woman even at the best of times but when my great-grandfather stood beside her they looked like a big gander and a little goose. She had never been a great talker but you could see from the way her eyes moved quickly like a pair of small fish, that she thought a great deal. So she stood there in an old torn black dress, with a red ribbon in her tightly curled black hair which always looked freshly oiled, and told them how she happened to blow up the bronze horse at Nevel.

The revolutionary party Aunt Chaya belonged to was not very large, but Aunt Chaya had been a member ever since she was a girl. In those days a few of the less religious youngsters from the village used to go in couples, the boys with red handkerchiefs tied round their necks, their arms round the waists of the girls, the girls with red ribbons in their hair, into the woods, there to listen to one another's speeches, and to sing revolutionary songs, and also, to be frank, to make love. One Sunday afternoon, Chaya, a young girl at the time, followed them into the wood, hid in a tree nearby, listened, watched and learned. Then she came down from the tree and said that unless they let her become a member she would tell all their fathers what the Revolution really meant. So they let her join although she was so small and so young, but soon they began to respect her. She had a genius for hiding revolutionary pamphlets. She became secretary of the group, and once when the police came to the village to see if there were any deserters from the tsar's army about, Chaya hid a broken pistol which a party speaker from Lutzen had given her. She hid it in an earth closet and all the brothers and sisters in the party said what a genius she had for organization. But when Chaya left the village and the others had all married, and the boys blew their noses or carried their dinners in the red handkerchiefs, and the girls used their red ribbons to tie their aprons, Chaya began to learn other things. She even went on missions and because the party remained so small, became a very important person indeed.

I am telling you all this so that you shouldn't be surprised that Aunt Chaya, small as she was, should be chosen to throw the bomb at Peter Petrovich Minsky. But now I expect you want to know something about Peter Petrovich as well, for there is no end to people's curiosity. So.

Peter Petrovich was a clerk in the recruitment office at Nevel. When the recruits were brought in, Peter Petrovich pulled his thick moustaches, stared through his steel-framed spectacles which contained only plain glass but which made him feel important, and asked questions. 'Your name is what?' —'You were born where?'—'Your father was what?' Naturally a man who asks so many questions is a great nuisance.

Aunt Chaya's party had just decided that the only way to be

noticed was to become a great nuisance just like Peter Petrovich. There he was, a very small official indeed, but if it wasn't
for Peter Petrovich there would be no recruitment office, and if
there was no office there would be nowhere for the recruits
to go to, and if there was nowhere for the recruits to go
to, they would have to stay home in their villages, and if
they stayed at home they wouldn't be in the tsar's army, and
then the tsar would have no army, and there would be nothing
to stop the revolution. If it wasn't for Peter Petrovich there
would be happiness for all and a picture of Aunt Chaya in
every village in Russia, but there was Peter Petrovich sitting
every day in his recruitment office, pulling his moustaches, looking through his plain glasses, asking questions and sending men
into the tsar's army. It was unbearable that such a man as he
should stand in the way of the revolution, and the party decided
it wouldn't put up with it any longer. Peter Petrovich was to
be blown up one morning as he went into his recruitment office.
The morning was better than the evening because there would
be more people about and this would make the bomb-thrower
harder to find. It would also save another day's lot of men from
the tsar's army. What was more natural than that Aunt Chaya
with her record and reputation should be chosen to throw the
bomb. Though my great-grandfather was against fighting
except sometimes with fists like a man, believe me, he (we all)
would have been insulted if Aunt Chaya had not been chosen.

Now the recruitment office of Peter Petrovich Minsky stood
in the market-place of Nevel, and in the centre of this market-
place there also stood a large beautiful very old bronze horse.
Tell me how many towns do you know where they have a
bronze horse? You agree, not every town in the world can turn
round and say 'We have a bronze horse standing in the market-
place.' And the bronze horse at Nevel was certainly a horse to

end horses. There it stood in the snow and in the heat, covered with ice or covered with dust, always at the centre of Nevel for everyone to see and admire. It pranced up, waving its forefeet in the air, its mane blew all over the place, its tail was long and thick, its thighs were enormous, its eyes were wild, its nostrils wide open, its teeth bared, its lips covered with spume. Why, you could almost hear it neighing, you could almost hear its hind-feet stamp the earth, and any minute it might run you over and leave Nevel behind in a cloud of dust. No wonder the citizens of Nevel were proud of that horse, for whoever you are it would have given you pleasure to see it. You would have taken your cap off to the town of Nevel and agreed that it was a very fine town indeed.

Peter Petrovich Minsky passed the bronze horse every day as he crossed the market-place to his recruitment office. Every day he walked past the horse without so much as a look at it, staring straight ahead through his glasses, counting up, no doubt, how many good men he would throw to the tsar that day. For all I know he got a commission on each man, per head, you might say, like cattle or sheep. Nevel could spare such a man and nothing more might have been said if only Aunt Chaya had been a little more careful. The fact is that in spite of her quick bright eyes she was a little bit long-sighted. Certainly Peter Petrovich must have been very annoyed at losing all his hair, especially his moustache, and of course his glasses were completely destroyed, and his office overcoat torn to shreds, but he himself was still alive after the bomb was thrown. But the bronze horse, Oh, my goodness, the bronze horse had really left Nevel in a cloud of dust. And when the dust cleared there was nothing to be seen except its hind-feet. Everything else was spread all over the market-place. A cabbage-seller was knocked out by one of the front legs, a stall of cakes was upset by its head, everything was in a terrible state, and the bronze horse had left Nevel for good. You can imagine how everyone felt about Aunt Chaya. Peter Petrovich they could manage without, but the bronze horse, who could forgive?

So it was with great enthusiasm that the police from Nevel began to make inquiries after Aunt Chaya. And, she said, it was only a matter of time before they traced her to the village. 'And to my house?' asked my great-grandfather. 'Exactly so,' replied Aunt Chaya, her eyes darting about the room looking for policemen.

Everyone started to shout and ask questions again and, naturally, my great-grandmother was crying. 'Well,' said my great-grandfather, 'let everyone be quiet. We are all in great danger and I must think carefully. But what, first of all, is that terrible smell?' Everyone turned round and sniffed, and my great-grandmother cried out, 'It must be the cat. She is dead you know.'

At this moment who should run in but a friend of my young grandfather's, a boy with a very long nose and side-curls, who was, in spite of being pious, a terrible liar. 'Listen,' he shouted, 'a whole lot of police are arriving on horses. Which is your Aunt Chaya who blew up the bronze horse at Nevel?'

'Oh, my God,' cried my great-grandfather, 'it is too late to do anything. Hide under the stove Chayele quickly, with the chickens, and perhaps they will not see you. What a terrible smell,' he went on, 'where is this dead cat?'

Now though it was really a bad smell, my great-grandfather was sorry to see the cat gone like that, for it was a good cat and had lived with the family for a long time, catching rats sometimes as long as your arm. All the children played with it and it hardly ever bit them except when rats were short, and this wasn't often because there were plenty of rats at all times in the village. It was not a cat to die so easily, brought up like that, to a hard life with few comforts. But what had happened was that by dying this cat actually saved eight lives. Now I expect you had better hear all about that before I finally explain how Aunt Chaya was buried.

It is a strange thing that among all the foods which the true believer may not eat you do not find mushrooms mentioned. And yet on the other hand it is not such a strange thing, because the rabbis must have known how good a pot of mushrooms can taste, and how they make a change from soup and potatoes. My great-grandmother's mother was very fond of a dish of mushrooms, so fond of them in fact, that in the season, in spite of being a very old woman—you can tell how old, she was my great-grandfather's mother-in-law—she would go down to the meadows and look around for perhaps two or three hours for mushrooms. In those days there were really mushrooms, not like now, the size of a pin-head, but big as saucers, big as plates some of them.

One morning the old woman was searching in some new fields, slowly walking along talking to herself, and looking carefully about—but she couldn't find her mushrooms anywhere. 'So,' she said, 'now they are taking from me my only pleasure. They take from an old woman a few mushrooms nobody wants. Nobody wants me. Nobody looks after me so they take away my mushrooms.' As she got ready to cry a little she suddenly noticed a whole dinner of mushrooms under some trees. 'My prayer has been answered,' she wheezed, 'there is a God who cares for the old and will never see them want.'

What wonderful mushrooms they were, bigger than ever before, and golden yellow like rich butter! Home she took them talking all the time and feeling like an angel. She skinned and washed them, flavoured them just so, and left the pot on the stove to cook while she sat in a corner and saw that no one took them away. But she was tired by the excitement and so much talking to herself, and fell asleep in no time. When, suddenly, there was a noise and the old woman woke up, it was already too late, for the cat had knocked the pot down and was eating the mushrooms up as quickly as she could swallow. How the old woman swore at the cat, and kicked it, and threw things at it, but it was too hungry to notice. Without moving it finished the mushrooms and then, leaving the old woman crying her eyes out lamenting the misery of being old and weak, the cat walked into my great-grandfather's workshop and went to sleep and died from fungus-poisoning in one of his biggest and warmest tool-chests.

So it was that this famished cat saved the old woman's life— such as there was left of it—as well as the lives of her grand-children, because, naturally, she always gave them a few spoon-fuls of her mushroom stew. And how everyone in the house knew it at last, for when my grandmother had seen the cat lying dead in the toolchest, and had said 'Aach', and closed the lid hoping somehow it would disappear. It did not disappear. It was smelling to the highest part of heaven which brings us back to the story of how Aunt Chaya was buried.

It turned out that this little liar, who, you remember, came rushing in shouting, 'The police are coming,' was telling the truth for a change. In next to no time the police were in the house, and everyone stood around with their mouth open, saying 'Sir' because this is the only way to make sure that a policeman doesn't take you to prison. Only two policemen came into the house but believe me, when you've got a hunted criminal hiding under the stove with the chickens, even two policemen are no joke. Furthermore outside could be heard the voices of a whole regiment swearing and laughing and telling dirty stories to one another.

One of the policemen must have been a general almost, for he was covered from head to foot in gold braid and gold lines and gold tassels. He had an enormous moustache—much bigger than Peter Petrovich's—and he kept his helmet on, which my great-grandmother thought was very nice of him, it being the custom in an orthodox house. The other policeman was less well-dressed but much fatter. He took his helmet off and called my great-grandmother 'Dear lady' and she didn't like the look of him at all. My great-grandfather just said good day to them, and beckoned all the children to leave the room.

The first policeman looked round the room and wrinkled his nose. 'Do you smell something unpleasant, Ruspensky?' he asked. The other replied, 'I do Peter Ilyitch. Are you the brother of the revolutionary Chaya?' he snapped at my great-grandfather.

'It is a deathly smell, Ruspensky,' said the other policeman, 'I believe——'

'Don't say it, Ruspensky,' answered Peter Ilyitch, 'I think you are right.' He turned on my great-grandfather and said sternly, 'There is something dead in this house is there not?' And truthfully my great-grandfather replied, 'There is.'

'And where is your sister Chaya, the red cow?' asked one of the two (I don't know whether Peter Ilyitch or Ruspensky). Praying silently my great-grandfather said, 'She has been dead these two days and in this hot weather, you understand. Please let me take you to the body so that you can arrest her, because if what I hear is true then she deserves to be sent to Siberia whether she is dead or not.'

The two policemen were crossing themselves again and again. 'Peter Ilyitch, we should never have come into this accursed place. We shall be cursed for ever—already I have a pain in my belly,' said Ruspensky.

'We must inspect the coffin, Ruspensky, or we cannot make a report,' replied Peter Ilyitch. 'Take us to it,' he ordered my great-grandfather.

When he had led them into his workshop, praying all the time, my great-grandfather said, 'Here is the coffin and accursed mortal remains of that devil's cat. There is truly a curse on them but perhaps you would care to inspect them?'

Now you must understand that the atmosphere in the workshop was really unbearable. The cat had been dead for maybe six or seven days in very hot weather, and there it had stayed, for business was too bad for my great-grandfather to bother to go into his workshop. And since it would be terrible bad luck, the last thing the police wanted was to examine my devilish Aunt Chaya's mortal remains. 'No,' he said, 'unnecessary. She smells dead enough, the witch. God—the pain in my belly is becoming terrible,' and he pushed Peter Ilyitch out of the house. 'Arrange to bury that malignant tomorrow, you,' he shouted to my great-grandfather. 'Certainly, my lord,' called my great-grandfather, 'with pleasure.' And he wiped his forehead on his sleeve.

Aunt Chaya remained under the stove throughout her burial. Very quickly it was whispered round the village what had happened, and naturally everyone was pleased to attend the burial service the next day. The cat in the tool-chest was carried up to the grave-yard with the whole village following behind my great-grandfather and three others carrying the box. The cantor was here and sang the whole service beautifully without a single interruption from my great-grandfather. Everyone wept, and after the last shovelful of earth had fallen they all shook hands and wished my great-grandfather and mother long life.

D

Meanwhile Ruspensky and Peter Ilyitch stood by on their horses. They both had headaches because the brandy at the inn where they stayed the night was so bad, and Ruspensky still had a terrible stomach-ache and knew he was accursed.

Everyone said what a pity it was that Aunt Chaya had to miss her burial. As for the cat, believe me, it was entitled to become a saint if we had such things. Anyhow it must surely have had the finest funeral any cat, believer or otherwise, has ever had anywhere. Even in Pinsk I bet they don't look after cats better.

A FOOL IS ESSENTIAL

IN A village there has to be a fool. Where everyone lives on top of everyone else there has to be someone with whom even the most foolish action will go unnoticed, someone, we will agree, who is more stupid than you or I. In my great-grandfather's village, anyone could always consider himself better off and more gifted than Simcha the Golem, as they called him. When someone was annoyed with his wife's cooking he could always laugh at the thought of what Simcha had to go through with his shrew of a woman. When the rabbi said something which my great-grandfather might nod his head against, at least Simcha took it for the word of God. So that quite certainly Simcha was a fool, as stupid as if his head were made of clay, but although everyone agreed that he was a fool, the son of a fool and the father of fools, they still liked him, because in a small village a fool is essential. He gives everyone a feeling of self-respect. 'At least I am better than Simcha the Golem, the fool, the clay-head.'

So, besides being a convenience for the village, what good was Simcha? If he wasn't bad it was only because he couldn't think of anything wrong to do, and after all, what we consider so good in a good man is the fact that if he chose he could be as evil as he is good. And everyone is grateful about it, because not being evil he doesn't steal your goods, interfere with your daughter, hurt your cow, or cheat you very much in business. But Simcha, oh, Simcha, you could never call good like this. He simply wasn't bad; he wasn't anything. But as sometimes happens with a man like Simcha, though his head was thick clay, his shoulders were an ox's, his legs as solid as the two

trees behind the synagogue, and his hands so knotted with
strength that he could straighten a horse-shoe as you can bend
a pin. And through this gift he made a living.

If you had a heavy parcel Simcha carried it. If a wagon
was stuck in the mud, when in the spring the snow and ice
were melting, Simcha would move it. If you were building a
house and collecting wood for it, Simcha would cut down the
trees as if they were saplings and carry the wood there for you.
Every day he worked like a beast except Saturday, for on the
Sabbath he went to the Synagogue. When he got there Simcha
stood behind all the other men just watching and watching, his
eyes moving from one face to another like a bird's. He listened
for as long as there was anything to listen to. When everyone
sat Simcha crouched on the floor, when they stood up, so did
he, and when some old men in the front row started to snuffle
and grunt 'Sha, sha,' to boys who were making a noise or other
old men who were discussing too loudly the right and wrongs
of some affair, Simcha would stand up at the back there, glare
around at everyone and shout 'SHA, SHA, SHA.' When everyone turned to look at him he grinned and blushed and sat down
again, for he was, in spite of his size, somewhat shy.

Though Simcha could never pray for himself he got very
near it by crying his eyes out and beating his breast harder
than anyone else in the synagogue. When he beat his breast it
made a hollow sound like a copper drum, and his tears fell like
heavy rain drops upon his fists. He forgot to follow the actions
of the men in all things but went on beating, beating, crying,
crying like a child all the time. Did Simcha know why he was
so upset? He didn't, but if so many good men were miserable
then he had to be miserable as well, just as when they were
happy shaking hands with their neighbours, the rabbi dancing
with the scrolls in his arms, hugged closely to him, Simcha

danced and made noises as if he too were happy. This was Simcha, a fool, a fool in a village like any other fool, harmless and with a body like iron, a servant to everyone.

Now this Simcha lived in a filthy hut with a woman who had no dowry. She was cross-eyed, her wig was never clean, and she hated everything. She hated Simcha most of all. So why did she marry him then? A wife should at least not hate a husband. But who else would have married her? She waited as long as she could and then, cursing all the men in the village, she married Simcha. What could he do to protect himself? When she spoke to him, he grinned. She went on speaking and he went on grinning, until she managed to grin back, making her cross-eyes smaller and stretching her mouth into a thick red worm. Simcha was finished. She married him, and he made a hut out of pieces of wood which nobody wanted and took her to live there, although after a few nights he began to sleep in the open again, except when the weather was too bad, not because he wanted to insult her but because in the hut he couldn't breathe.

Every day of the year you could hear his wife cursing Simcha the Golem. As the years passed her only pleasure was to stand in the door of the hut with her children climbing around her, all cursing Simcha at the tops of their voices. But still he went on working to bring them a few kopecks, and still he always looked surprised when he gave them to her and she cursed him for it. People sometimes gave him a little more when they thought of his sorrow. He thanked them as he always did, gave the money to his wife as usual, and she cursed him again. She never grinned at him any more. Perhaps it was an accident that she ever did.

If Sholem Pinsk wanted above all to go to the city of Pinsk where he pretended he had already been, if the rabbi wanted above all to be visited by an angel, if Yaacov the teacher's son wanted only to print something in a paper, then it is reasonable that Simcha should want something also. You would see him sometimes sitting by the road smoking tea-leaves wrapped in newspaper. He pressed the leaves together into the shape of one of his own thick fingers, wrapped them carefully, and smoked them, a dreamy look on his face, staring at the road yet seeing nothing but what—what is the dream of such a fool? Tea-leaves he collected every day from the inn, straight from the big urn where tea was always brewing. He dried them in a little heap on the stove and put them in his pocket. As he left the inn he watched men smoking their pipes quietly and the same dreamy look came over his face as when he smoked his own newspaper cigars by the roadside.

Once when Simcha was drying tea-leaves on the stove my great-grandfather came into the inn. He sat down with a glass of brandy, for it was a market-day and he had sold one or two pipes. He got out his own pipe, one which he had made when he got married to celebrate and to soothe him. He filled it with tobacco from a leather bag, and sat smoking quietly. Then he noticed Simcha was staring at him, and he said:

'Good day to you Simcha. Have you made a good meal?'

For how else can you talk to a simple man other than about the things that mean something in his life? Yet Simcha did not reply. He stared at my great-grandfather for a while, then suddenly stood up and left, his face black and miserable.

'What have you said to Simcha?' asked a man.

'Nothing at all,' replied my great-grandfather. 'He is surly, a surly fool. Whenever he sees me he looks like that. Have I got the evil eye?'

'What do you expect from a fool?' replied the man.

Yet Simcha had no ill-feeling for my great-grandfather. The

sight of a pipe always made him sad, and the sight of a pipe-maker smoking his own pipe, a pipe which made all others look small and badly carved, made poor Simcha more miserable than a regiment of cross-eyed wives, more weary than twenty wagons of corn, more black in the face than insults, more cold through his whole body than the darkest winter. Because he did not understand any of these things Simcha simply accepted them when they came, but a pipe—ah, a pipe he had wanted all his life, so that the mere sight of my great-grandfather's pipe made him feel sick and empty. Desire came suddenly upon him and he felt weak in his guts.

As Simcha smoked his tea-leaves quietly by the roadside he dreamed of a pipe. Pipes filled his mind and his dream was happy, until all other pipes were cleared away and a pipe of my great-grandfather's making lay in the mind of Simcha with nothing else at all. Simcha moved his fingers stroking its warm bowl. His thick fingers moved gently as if handling a moth.

So in the life of Simcha, which was simply one thing after another exactly as it happened, this was the only misery. And things grew worse with him. When he lay down at night he looked up at the sky and it was nothing to him. He carried bigger packs, he pushed more wagons out of the mud, his children spat at him, his neighbours laughed, yet he, he thought only of a pipe. He talked less and less for 'pipe' was the only word he wanted to say, and to what purpose? But he spent as much time as he could near my great-grandfather's workshop watching, always watching. He saw the pipes being made, and as the stock piled up Simcha rejoiced. But as the pipes sold he grew sad, so sad he would not work but lay on his back all day moping. The taste went out of his newspaper cigars. His life went out as all men lit their new pipes and sighed their contentment.

My great-grandfather wasn't blind. He saw Simcha watching him, but he went on with his work. If a fool wants to watch, let him, it was none of his business. But after a while he had to admit that his shaping and carving were not as good as they had been. He cursed his tools, he hit my young grandfather for no reason at all, yet still as he bent over his bench he felt the blank eyes of Simcha the Golem watching him. His blood began to boil in his veins, his neck grew red, his eyes became bloodshot. Then one day when in the hot sunshine Simcha just stood looking and looking not saying a word, my great-grandfather swept everything off his bench, and with a shout threw down his tools.

Simcha stood still, but his eyes were suddenly full of tears. He rushed up to the bench and searched all around it muttering to himself and crying.

My great-grandfather shouted, 'Are you satisfied now, you great fool? Are you satisfied? Standing there loafing, looking with big cow's eyes all day long. Are you satisfied?'

Simcha said nothing. Then he found the broken bowl of the pipe my great-grandfather had been working on, and his tears fell like rain as he held the two pieces together.

'Simcha,' said my great-grandfather more quietly. 'What is the matter?'

Simcha opened his mouth, holding the pieces out towards my great-grandfather. His lips tried to make words and his tongue went in and out, but he said nothing.

'Tell me what's wrong Simcha. Are you in pain?'

'A pipe—a pipe I want.' Through the thick lips came a voice as small as a little cat.

'Take one then, Simcha, you should have spoken before. Have one, certainly, any one you like,' said my great-grandfather.

Simcha looked down at the broken pipe in his hand. He wiped his face with his fist. The pipe was carved with a bull's head; you could mark out its fierce eyes and its nostrils, and the powerful muscles of its thick neck below the bowl.

'A bull,' said Simcha, and he turned away and went and sat by the roadside. He placed the two pieces of the broken pipe on the grass together and without looking away from them took a packet out of his pocket. He opened the packet, took out tea-leaves and newspaper, and rolled a cigar as thick as one of his own stupid fingers.

'Have a good pipe, Simcha, have one of these,' shouted my great-grandfather.

Simcha looked at the bull's-head pipe on the grass. He put the cigar between his lips and lit it without ever looking away from the two pieces of the pipe. His face looked just as the rabbi's face would look if suddenly an angel came up the village street and told him that next year it would be in Jerusalem.

THE PORTRAIT

NOT very many strangers came to my great-grandfather's village, but when it happened everyone knew and avoided them, not that they felt unfriendly, but because usually strangers came from the police or the army or the tax-collectors, and who wants to talk to such people?

So it was when early one spring, just as the snow and ice were beginning to disappear, a stranger arriving in the village walked about all day trying to start conversations, without anyone answering more than 'Yes' or 'No', and sometimes even less. Now this stranger carried a box on his back, and wore his beard trimmed close to his face. He was a big man, too, and what with his red neck and the black beard he looked like a bull. He walked about the village the whole day, sometimes pulling out a book to write something, and smiling at people when they unsmiling hurried past him, until at last he began to feel that perhaps no one liked him very much. Just as he came to this conclusion he happened to be walking past my great-grandfather's workshop.

My great-grandfather bent over his bench working a piece of wood into the shape of a pipe-bowl. Though he didn't look up, he saw the stranger, and furthermore, he saw the stranger take out his book and write something in it. As he wrote, the stranger looked up every so often at my great-grandfather's workshop until my great-grandfather decided that even if the man watching him was a tax-collector he should at least know what he was going to get into trouble for. So he put down his chisel, and went outside.

The stranger watched him as he walked up to the gate

slowly. My great-grandfather considered meanwhile which would be the best way to address the foreigner. Should he call him plain 'Sir' or 'Your lordship' or what? But before he could decide, the man ran up the path towards him shouting. He clapped his arms round my great-grandfather and shouted right in his ear:

'I have searched Russia for this face!'

And the stranger embraced my great-grandfather before anything could be done to stop him, still shouting, 'My God— this is the face I have been looking for!'

By this time my great-grandfather realized he was dealing with a madman, so doing his best not to make things worse by seeming not to want the embrace of the man, he got himself out from his grip, and walked back a few paces. The madman stood there with his arms stretched out, a stupid smile on his face, looking like a bull smiling, and he said happily:

'I never expected to find such a face in such a village as this, never.'

Though he didn't quite see why a face as his shouldn't be found in his own village, my great-grandfather decided not to argue with the madman about that. Instead he said to him, 'If you don't mind my asking you, what are you embracing me for?' To which the man replied, 'I have always known this face in my mind. Only now for the first time I have seen it.'

Which made my great-grandfather think, 'Who wants to argue with a madman?' Though he said, 'Well, I'm glad you like it, but if you don't want to buy a pipe now I'll go back to my workshop.' And he turned to go back into his workshop.

Before he could walk more than two or three yards the man rushed up to him and shouted again like at first, 'You must let me have it!'

By now my great-grandfather was getting a little annoyed,

because he was always a man with a quick temper. Once he lost his temper with anyone it was not such a good thing for that person. But still he kept polite and said to the madman:

'Please. You only just now said to me that you liked my face and you didn't want to buy a pipe. Now you want it. Either you want to buy a pipe or you do not want to buy a pipe. I don't mind which.' And he pushed the man's hand from off his shoulder.

But the madman wouldn't go. Again he said, 'You must let me have it. You must give me your face.'

This was altogther too much for my great-grandfather. He turned away saying, 'Please do me a favour and stop making jokes with me. I am a poor man with work to do.' And he walked away quickly.

Yet still the madman—he must have been really mad—wouldn't leave him alone. He shouted—he was always shouting—'I only mean you should let me paint a picture of you.'

My great-grandfather, who had never seen a picture of himself, stopped with his back towards the madman—who was perhaps not so mad after all. He thought of a picture of himself which everyone could see and recognize and point at and say, 'Look at that! Isn't it him to the very life? You know who that is? He is the finest pipe-maker in all Russia.' Why shouldn't there be a picture of him? After thinking which he turned round and asked, 'Why should you want to paint me? And how much would you charge?'

The madman, who was (as you can tell) really an artist, answered very quickly, 'Believe me, my good sir, it would be a pleasure and a privilege for me to paint your portrait for nothing.'

Which made my great-grandfather wonder whether there was something else behind it after all. But when he told the artist, 'I wouldn't be able to have a painted image made in my own house. I'm a religious man, you must realize,' the artist said, 'You shouldn't worry about that. I will paint the picture here in your own front yard and everyone in the village shall see it, and then with your permission I will take it back to the city for other people to see.'

So my great-grandfather said to himself, 'If people want to see my painted picture and this madman wants to paint my picture, why should I make so many people disappointed? After all, this madman is no fool. Hasn't he picked me from among everyone in the village?' And he replied to the man, 'All right then. I give you my kind permission to paint me.'

To which the artist answered, very excited, 'Thank you, thank you. Let us begin now.'

My great-grandfather, never having had his portrait painted before, said, 'All right, then. Paint.' And he turned for the third time to go back into the house. But the artist explained to him that he had to sit still for a while, and after a lot of fuss they brought out a small piece of wood for putting the paints on, and all the other things which he used for painting. There were so many of these things I haven't got the time to tell you all about them. But what does it matter? However many things there were they were needed for painting my great-grandfather's portrait.

The artist, who was a quick workman, finished the painting in a couple of hours, and all the time my great-grandfather kept asking him, 'Well, is it finished? How much longer?'

But the artist was so polite and told him so many times that this was the face he had been looking for everywhere, that my great-grandfather sat more or less still the whole time, thinking about how the village would be surprised, and what the rabbi would say, and how jealous Reb Sholem Pinsk would be that the artist had not asked him if his face could be painted. Of course, my great-grandmother was also there, standing near my great-grandfather hoping that the artist might be painting her into the picture as well. As for my young grandfather, he had run round to all the houses telling them what was happening, so that more and more people crowded round the artist as he sat on his little stool painting. My young grandfather stood in the front of the crowd shouting out, 'Now he's painting the nose. Now he's painting the eye.' And so on until the artist had finished, when my grandfather shouted out, 'Now he's finished!'

Then the whole crowd, which had been watching very quietly, breathed out together, and no wonder, because the painting was the first one which had ever been made in the village, and what do you think? It looked exactly like my great-grandfather even to the eyes, one of which was brown while the other was blue. Reb Sholem Pinsk, however, was speaking in a loud high voice, saying, 'Such excitement over a little picture like this! In Pinsk everyone is painted, not little like this, but big—almost as big as a house.'

But no one took any notice because Reb Sholem was the only one who had seen pictures in Pinsk or anywhere else, and no one believed that he had been to Pinsk anyhow.

When my great-grandmother saw the picture she was at first very upset because she wasn't in it. She said, 'How could he leave me out? Wasn't I standing there right beside the bench?'

Still, when she saw all the other women looking at the picture first up close and after from a little distance away, she decided it was indeed a proud moment for her. She stood beside the picture for the whole time it was in the yard with the crowd around it, smiling to everyone and bowing her head as if she had painted it herself. Oh, there was no doubt about it, the picture was very fine indeed, although my young grandfather was in the back-yard having a fight with a boy who said it looked like the Tsar Nicholas himself. Everyone agreed the picture was a wonderful likeness except Reb Sholem, who kept asking, 'Will anyone tell me whose picture this is? It is no doubt a very fine likeness, but surely it is no one in this village.'

However, who listened to him? They were all standing around my great-grandfather waiting there to shake him by the hand, to congratulate him and wish him long life. Everyone told the artist how clever he was, and the rabbi asked him if he wasn't grateful to God for such a gift to be breathed into his hands, to which the artist replied that he most certainly was very grateful. Then Reb Sholem asked him how much a man could earn in the city making pictures like this, to which the artist replied, 'No money could buy a picture like this.'

My great-grandfather smiled, and poured out brandy for everyone, while my young grandfather looked round to see if any more of the boys felt like saying the picture was a bad likeness.

Well, the artist stayed in the house of my great-grandfather that night, as guest of honour, though the picture was left in the workshop because, as the rabbi pointed out, even such a good picture as this was in a sense a graven image and could not be kept in an orthodox house. My great-grandmother made a special borscht which was so thick it could be cut in slices, and there were plenty of potatoes as well. After everyone else had gone to bed, the artist stayed up talking with my great-grandfather. They finished another bottle of brandy, though what they talked about I do not know, because my grandfather was asleep on top of the stove at the time and consequently did not hear, and therefore was not able to tell me.

The next day the artist went. Everyone saw him off from the village. Afterwards they spent days talking about what an honour it was for the village that my great-grandfather had been painted. Pity the artist took the picture away with him, wrapped up in cloth my great-grandmother cut from one of her best petticoats. A picture like that could only be wrapped in the best. It was nice too that after the artist had left and my great-grandmother looked about the house, she could find nothing missing, which may have been because she had hidden away the silver sticks for the candles used on holidays and Friday evenings, and there was nothing else to steal in the house except the hens, which she then counted and found all present. It was, however, this artist and what happened to the silver candlesticks which he did not steal that brought the great shame of his life on my great-grandfather. This shame was not to fall for several months, but it did fall, and when it fell it was a very great shame indeed.

What happened was this. Later on, in the same year as my great-grandfather had his portrait painted, my young grandfather was sent to the market to buy some fish cheap. This market was held in the village over the hill where they were celebrating a holiday called Lent in which for some reason or other everyone goes crazy and eats fish the whole time. There was therefore a lot of fish on sale. Though there were also stalls with fruit, vegetables, and even a few selling spindles—which they make out of soft wood which grows in the forests near my great-grandfather's village—and a stall with toys. Still almost all the stalls sold fish. Which means, since the peasants can catch their own fish, that it will be sold cheaply. So my young grandfather was sent over there to buy some fish, although when he returned out of breath and red in the face, he had, strange to say, brought no fish with him. When my great-grandmother asked where the fish was, he couldn't answer he was so excited and out of breath. Even when she asked him for the second time, 'So, where is the fish, you little loafer?' he still found it hard to reply, though in the end he managed to answer, 'In the market there is a stall covered with pictures of my father.' At which my great-grandmother could hardly believe her ears. She put on her best shawl, and told my grandfather, 'If this is only one of your stories I shall see to it that you are sorry for it. Telling your mother stories!'

But he replied to her, 'Come and see for yourself then. I am telling you—a stall is covered with big and small pictures of my father.' And he led my great-grandmother back to the market at a terrible pace.

When she got there my great-grandmother walked through the crowds looking all round, my grandfather following eating an apple which he had found near a stall which happened to be selling apples. When he was about to eat the core, my great-grandmother stopped, turned round and said to him, 'Can I see this stall with pictures anywhere? Am I blind?'

My grandfather was so annoyed at not being believed the whole time, he threw away what was left of the apple-core—there was very little—swallowed what was in his mouth, and shouted, 'How do you expect to find it? Are you leading me or am I leading you? If you will only let me show the way instead of running everywhere like a squirrel, I will show you this stall with pictures of my father on it.' He was very annoyed.

Then he ran ahead so fast that my great-grandmother had trouble keeping sight of him. At last she saw him stop at a little stall at the end of the market. She hurried towards it promising herself she would see he had some of the nonsense knocked out of him even if he had told her the truth for a change. But she stopped before she got up to him. She stopped because on a large banner hung across the stall was a big ikon. And the face of the ikon—God should have forbidden it—was the face of my pious great-grandfather.

She was even more shocked when on coming closer to the stall she found that *all* the faces of *all* the ikons on the stall were the face of my great-grandfather. Big ikons or little ones, there was no difference in the faces, and each one of them had the name of a different saint written underneath it, though of course they were not different saints, they were all my great-grandfather.

Well, my great-grandmother blushed for shame. That a pious man like my great-grandfather should have a thing like this happen to him! She didn't wait to ask the orthodox man who kept the stall any questions. She ran straight back to the workshop to tell my great-grandfather, though she remembered to shout as she passed my grandfather that he should buy some fish.

While his mother was away my grandfather went back to the apple stall to see if he could find any more apples. On the way he met a friend, and they decided that my grandfather should find apples while his friend asked the peasant whose stall it was how much he would take for six pounds of apples. After they had done this, the friend explained at length to the peasant that the apples were too dear, they went to a quiet part of the market and ate the apples which my grandfather had carried away in the legs of his trousers which were tied at the outside with string.

Meanwhile my great-grandmother was explaining what she had seen to my great-grandfather, who was (as you might expect) struck dumb by the news. He was unable to think, so full was his mind of big and small ikons, all with his face painted on them. Then he saw with his mind's eye Reb Sholem

Pinsk holding these ikons close to his face to see them properly, then looking round and laughing and rubbing his hands, telling everyone in the world about this great shame that had fallen upon my great-grandfather. After watching such things in his mind for so long that my great-grandmother thought he was never going to answer, he pulled on his coat, and rushed out of the house without a word.

My great-grandfather hurried to the market, found the stall and stood dumbly looking at the ikons. While he wondered what to do, my grandfather was still eating apples with his friend, and already they were beginning to feel slight pains in the stomach though they still went on eating. My great-grandfather at last decided that all he could do was buy the ikons and bury them. He was about to speak to the orthodox man who kept the stall when the man said to him, 'Haven't I met you somewhere, in Lutzen perhaps? I seem to know your face. Yes, yes, it is Mendel the Carrier, surely.'

My great-grandfather said no, he was not Mendel the Carrier. He was in fact a pipe-maker, and he would like to buy all the ikons on the man's stall. The man looked in amazement and said: 'What should an orthodox man with such side-curls be doing with all these images, and anyhow, can any man be so religious as to want so many ikons?'

My great-grandfather said to him not to mind, that he wanted to make presents to all the peasants who were his customers, and that the man should make him a fair price for all the ikons. Well, naturally they argued for a long time, the man explaining that he had paid a big price for them but that's how he was in business—he always paid too much for his goods, still, seeing as my great-grandfather was such a generous fellow he would only ask him for six roubles for the whole lot complete.

'What? Six roubles? Am I made of money?' inquired my great-grandfather.

The man said all right, it was a terrible loss to him but he would take five roubles. Eventually, when my great-grandfather offered him two roubles, he said it was robbery but he would take three roubles and a pipe. All my great-grandfather had to do now was to find three roubles, and from where was he going to get so much money? A man can work a whole week and keep a family on a rouble so where was he going to get three roubles from? There was only one man who could spare so much money in the village—Asher the Moneylender, but you think Asher was a moneylender because he was fond of giving people money? No. Asher always had to have something of yours as security before he could give you any money, and what had my great-grandfather got which might be a security for three roubles? I have already mentioned them. He had a pair of silver candlesticks for the Sabbath and for holidays.

Now a man may sell his animals or his piece of land or his cherry trees. He may even pawn his book if he has one, or his wife's beads or anything else he likes, but he may not pawn his silver candlesticks. He may not pawn them because they are not really his. They belong to his father, and to his son and to his son's son, and how will he keep the sabbath without his candlesticks, where will his wife put the candles so that she can light them when the sun goes down, and everyone can sit around the table, and say prayers, and eat supper with the candles burning on the table, and people passing outside seeing the light from the candles and everyone looking forward to worshipping God and doing no work the next day? Obviously a man can't pawn or sell his silver candlesticks. Without them his carry-on can fall to pieces. But in spite of this my great-grandfather was thinking about pawning his candlesticks. He asked himself which was the greater shame, to do that or to be in every peasant's hut under false pretences as Saint This and Saint That. While he could work to get back the candlesticks, what could he do to make up for being a saint under false pretences in the peasants' huts?

So he regretfully wrapped up the candlesticks in his coat and went out to pawn them, leaving my great-grandmother crying in the kitchen. He knew Asher never spoke about who came to him for money, but the whole way over to Asher's house he saw himself on pieces of wood hanging up in the corners of cottages all over Russia with lights burning in front of him and peasants praying to him. Believe me, it was far better to pawn the candlesticks, even if it was the greatest shame that ever fell upon my great-grandfather.

After he had seen Asher the Moneylender and argued about how much the candlesticks were worth, been offered a rouble, then two roubles, he finally took three and a half roubles, promising to pay Asher back four—because this after all, was how Asher made his living—my great-grandfather rushed back to the market where the orthodox man had already tied up all the ikons into a big parcel. He gave the parcel to my great-grandfather and said to him, 'For such a man as you who will spend money to make the peasants happy, I have a special gift.' And he handed him a little crucifix which he swore was made out of wood from the original cross.

All this time my grandfather was still with his friend and as they rubbed their stomachs they said what rotten apples the peasants sold, and how they made a mistake to bother to steal them. My great-grandfather didn't notice them but took the parcel home, putting the little crucifix in his pocket. He took the ikons into his workshop to wait until night came when he could bury them. All the while my great-grandmother still cried in the kitchen, lamenting the loss of the candlesticks, for how could my great-grandfather ever pay Asher back, and why had such a shame fallen upon the family and upon the whole village?

All day my great-grandfather would not eat. He spoke to no one and did no work. At last he came to the conclusion that somehow or other he must get his money back for the ikons—he simply couldn't afford to bury three roubles and the family candlesticks. But how to do it? He thought and thought and at last came to a solution. He sat up all night carving small faces out of soft wood. Though they weren't very good likenesses of anyone you could see they were faces. These he nailed onto the ikons, and then packed the whole lot up again. He would take them the very next day to the market, and sell them—a brilliant plan of campaign.

Which is what he did. But when he got to the market and set out the ikons, none of the peasants fancied them. My great-grandfather stood there with my young grandfather, feeling more and more certain he would never get back the candlesticks, my great-grandmother would cry in the kitchen for years without stopping. He got so tired of waiting to sell an ikon, even one, that he went off for a glass of brandy to help him forget his troubles. He drank two or three brandies, but with each drink he only felt his troubles more and more. He began to sing a song to cheer himself up, but in spite of the fact it was a drinking-song and consequently very happy, he began to cry a little, the tears dropping onto his beard. At last he decided he was wasting more money sitting there drinking only to get more miserable. He left the inn and found his way back to where my young grandfather was looking after the ikons.

When he finally got there my great-grandfather rubbed his

eyes in amazement. What should he see but my young grand-father lying on the ground sleeping with not a single ikon left. My great-grandfather knew at once they had all been stolen, he had done right to get more miserable. It was his great bad luck to have only such a boy as my grandfather to leave in charge of things. He pushed him with his foot, shouting:

'You fool, you! What have you done with all the ikons? You have let them get stolen while you sleep.'

My young grandfather jumped up and shouted right back, 'What do you think this is, then?' He shook his pockets and they jingled like mad. Then he took money out of them and gave it to my great-grandfather.

When my great-grandfather realized that the candlesticks were saved, he wept over my grandfather and blessed him, and finally asked him how this miracle had happened to them. My grandfather explained.

'I hung the ikons upside down one by one. A religious peasant may not see a saint treated like that. They bought to save them from being hung upside down.'

Still weeping my great-grandfather thanked God for such a son and went at once to Asher the Moneylender.

But at the same time, although everything came out all right in the eleventh hour, it was a shame on the family that even for a day the sabbath candlesticks should be in pawn.

THE DEVIL AND THE COW

NATURALLY my great-grandmother had a cow. Not that it was in any way a particularly good cow. It never won any prizes, it sometimes didn't give so much milk, one of its horns had got knocked off, and it would never come when it was called. It was an ordinary cow, a cow like any other, and when my great-grandmother went out at night to call, 'Masha, Masha,' (because that was its name) she might hear a noise somewhere, of something kicked over, but whether Masha heard my great-grandmother is another matter, because she never answered.

She wandered about all day and at night wandered still, into other people's yards, the street, a ploughed field, all night through, yet never tiring. Sometimes you would see Masha slowly walking over the hill. Those nights it took hours to find her again, and it was no use calling. As a further aggravation, this cow often went up to the ruin on top of the hill and stayed there all day.

You might say, 'All right, then, it was an annoying cow. What do you expect from a cow?'

But then you will have missed the whole point. It was an annoying cow, agreed, but going up to the ruins and loafing around them all day and night is too much, because, you understand, there was a devil up there.

This, of course, is the reason why my great-grandmother's cow gave so little milk. Not because she had a hard time being driven about the place all day, or because she never got enough to eat, but because two or three times a week she went up the hill to the ruins, and while she was there, the devil milked her.

So you will perhaps now agree that Masha was going too far, for who was going to climb a hill simply to be pushed down by a devil? No one would go after Masha.

No one, that is, except my great-grandmother, for she had to cook dinner every day, she had to find something to eat, and for this Masha was essential.

My great-grandmother used to ask the rest of them, 'Has anyone seen this devil? What does he look like? Like Sholem Pinsk, maybe? Or like your father when he was drunk last time?'

And so she went out every evening to find the cow, and even if it had gone up to the ruins she climbed the hill slowly, calling, 'Masha, Masha'. And though it happened she went up the hill many times to bring Masha back to the house, my great-grandmother never once saw that devil.

But that is not to say there was no devil to be seen. The time came when even my great-grandmother discovered that the devil was actually there, although even then she didn't exactly see him. Why should the devil waste his time showing himself to my great-grandmother? The devil is too busy to spend his time showing off to anyone who happens to walk up a hill looking for a lost cow. He lived there because he had a very good reason. If not, why should he waste his time at the top of such a little hill when there were so many mountains he could have chosen?

This devil could, in fact, have stayed wherever he fancied, like any other devil, but he chose the hill because of the ruins that were at the top of it. And it was not only the ruins that interested him, but what was hidden in them. Somewhere in those ruins was buried a treasure worth more than the whole village, more than Pinsk, even. No one knew what this treasure was exactly, but it had been hidden in the ruins for many years, and since every one said that there was a treasure, there certainly must have been one.

You might wonder why if there was a treasure no one tried to find it. After all, it's something, the chance of finding a fortune and living in a palace for the rest of your life, with servants around you and nothing to do except drink lemon tea and eat chicken all day long. And, naturally, several people had thought that it wouldn't be such a bad thing to find a treasure like this. But then, there was always the devil protecting it.

What is more, everyone knew the treasure could only be discovered at midnight by the light of a full moon. Why, they were unable to say, but that it was so no one questioned. Who would bother to invent such a ridiculous story? It was obviously true, and no matter how much someone wants a fortune it's not worth his while if it means being eaten by a devil. Even a dead lion is worth only the value of his skin, and believe me, not many people are buying lion skins these days.

So this was the situation—at the top of the hill there was a ruin, and in this ruin there was a treasure, and over this treasure there was sitting, or sometimes, maybe, standing or dancing—after all, a devil is a devil—a pretty dangerous devil. Anyone who thought of trying to find the treasure thought first of the devil, and then went out to earn an honest living instead.

For most people it would have been enough to know all this. Most people can be relied upon to act sensibly if they know that it will be a lot easier for them if they do—after all, a devil is a pretty good warning. However, sometimes you come across a man who just won't learn, and then there's no use talking. You must simply take no notice of such men. When they say, 'I think I'll go up to the ruin and take the treasure,' you simply reply, 'Good luck to you. You should have a nice night for it.' And then go about your business.

There is such a man in every village and this man is not necessarily large. In my great-grandfather's village he was small and thin, and although he lived in an orthodox village he wasn't orthodox but lived there because he had inherited a piece of land. This man was a carpenter and his name was Igor.

Igor never swore. He drank very little, yet he was certainly the most reckless man in the village. Sometimes he turned very quiet. Then suddenly he would disappear, coming back a couple of days later with a few dead wolves. Once he came back after a week with a bear-skin.

One night this Igor dug up the whole of the village street without saying a word to anyone. Suddenly one morning he was found standing there, with the whole street dug up. Being a reasonable man he put all the rubbish back when it was pointed out to him that the road being dug up made it difficult for people to pass. That was the sort of thing he used to do, yet in spite of this, everyone took him their trade, when they happened to need a coffin. Igor made good plain coffins of a seasoned wood which did not, like your cheap coffins, rot away in no time. Igor's coffins would last you a lifetime.

Mind, sometimes you felt uncomfortable meeting him, for as a result of measuring up so many people for their coffins, he always looked you up and down, working out how much timber you would need, and that sort of look makes you feel a little cold, particularly if lately you haven't been feeling too well.

This Igor may have been reckless when he dug up the village street for no reason at all, but, at least, there was—if the constable was not around—no danger in that. But when he suddenly came into my great-grandfather's workshop and said, 'I think that I shall go and find the treasure up on the hill,' it was something different. After all, what man, even if he is very strong, can hope to do well against a devil? A man is a man, and when he starts interfering with his betters, his chances of doing good business are worth a blown-out egg.

But that is what Igor said, and my great-grandfather could see he meant it. So after drinking a few glasses of brandy together, they shook hands and Igor went off to wait until the moon came up.

That very night my great-grandmother's cow decided to loaf about as usual. Still Igor wasn't a man to worry whether a skinny old cow was either here or there. He did what he had to do, regardless of cows and other people.

That night he took a few more brandies as he put the finishing touches to a beautiful coffin he was making for a small, very square, fat man he had studied with interest for some time. It was a good coffin and was sure to come in handy. When he had finished both the coffin and the bottle of brandy, he went out to the foot of the hill.

At the same time my great-grandmother was calling from her yard, 'Masha, Mashkele! Where are you, darling?' She knew the cow never answered, but she also could be stubborn.

Igor went up the hill, and once or twice he thought he heard someone calling, but he didn't look back. He went straight up towards the ruins and settled down to wait on a bank of grass with bushes growing on it, for midnight to come. My great-grandmother called out again after the cow, 'What are you doing, then?'

This time Igor heard. He stood up, all on guard. Again she cried, 'Well, why do you wait you beast?' Igor shouted back, 'You are the beast, you old devil.'

Now, when my great-grandmother heard a voice reply, she realized something unusual was going on. Masha the cow never answered, she never cared who waited for her, and here for the first time, a voice replied to my great-grandmother, calling her an old devil, into the bargain.

My great-grandmother was not the woman to stand for insults. At once she shouted back, 'I shall flay you alive, you dog!'

And this made Igor—who was a little drunk—remember what he had heard about the devil. Igor felt, for the first time, afraid. Nevertheless, he was determined to find the treasure, so he climbed quickly up the wall of the ruin and began to feel around the top of it with one hand, while holding onto the stones with the other.

My great-grandmother was by now beginning to worry about Masha, and she shouted as she walked up the hill, 'Where are you, little skinny beast?'

At this insult Igor—who was, you will remember, a little thin man—turned round to shout back, and saw, just below him, a single horn sticking up, and a great face with a dribbling mouth looking at him. At that very moment my great-grandmother shouted, 'I shall make you sorry you climbed up there.'

Now Igor was more than plain worried. He knew he was as good as dead. Wondering if they would bury him in the square coffin he had made for the fat man, he fell down into the long grass crying out, 'The devil is eating me!'

My great-grandmother could tell from all this racket that there was someone on the hill, and even she felt a little afraid. Then suddenly she saw a black shape charging towards her, because, just for a change, Masha had decided to move in the right direction for once.

My great-grandmother turned and ran, thinking that even if it wasn't actually the devil chasing her, a good woman couldn't be too careful, and whatever it was, she didn't like it. She ran all the way back home, and locked the door, waking everyone up.

My young grandfather looked out from on top of the stove where he slept. 'The devil played monkey-tricks with me,' cried his mother as all the chickens flew out from under the stove, kicking up a terrible fuss.

My great-grandfather looked very grave when he heard the whole story. 'You, running about the countryside all night like a madwoman shouting out, "Masha, Mashkele,"' he said. 'You should be ashamed. I suppose now you'll believe clever men who say there is a devil here or a devil there? Have a little respect in future.' And he went out to collect Igor's mortal remains.

When Igor told him how he had seen gold and jewels shining in the moonlight, my great-grandfather asked him if he had perhaps managed to bring a little away. He was very disappointed when he heard that just as Igor was about to reach out for the treasure, the jealous devil pushed him down and spat on him.

But as he wisely observed, 'At least it proves there must certainly be a treasure up in the ruins. For if not, why should the devil push you down? The devil is not a person to waste his time pushing people around for no reason.'

Igor sadly replied, 'If there was not a devil I would have got the treasure. A poor man can do no right.'

As for Masha, no one knew what became of her that night, though she came back the following day. My great-grandmother noticed she didn't look as pleased with herself as usual. Of course she still gave very little milk, but it was welcome. And of course she still refused to come when called. But after this my great-grandmother said she didn't care. For her part, the cow could loaf around the ruins every night if she liked. She could stay there and be roasted, for all my great-grandmother cared.

BONIFAS THE COBBLER

BONIFAS the Cobbler died when my grandfather was six. He died drunk in a puddle. That is to say, his face was in the puddle though the rest of him was lying across the road. And the rain came down for two or three days, and no one went out very much, and those that did said when they saw Bonifas in the road, 'That drunken peasant Bonifas! Let him get wet, the pig.'

And they walked over him to wherever they were going, but if they had tried to wake him up they would have been unlucky, because he was dead.

This Bonifas was a big peasant, very strong, with hands which could bend a horse-shoe straight, and though he was always drinking too much, he was a good cobbler. If you went to him and said, 'Look here, Bonifas, I would like a good pair of boots before the next holidays,' he would very likely be a little drunk, and then if he didn't try to beat your head with his hammer, he would laugh a great deal and keep clapping you across the back, and dribble onto his chin, which was even worse because he was still likely to hit you with his hammer. Or he might pick up a horse-shoe—there were always a few horse-shoes about his workshop for the purpose—and insist that you bet him a few kopecks he couldn't bend it straight. It was no use telling him he was maybe the strongest man in Russia, that he could bend anything he wanted, he still insisted, which cost you money for nothing. Of course, you could always refuse to bet, but it was advisable not to because he would shout, 'Oho —you call me a liar to my face! Where is my hammer?'

In this way then, Bonifas made a good living with which to

drink himself to death. But it was not only drinking that killed
this Bonifas. It was his behaviour when drunk. He would stand
in the middle of the village—and it wasn't his village either,
because he lived over the hill in the other place—he would
stand there shouting out terrible things while everyone who
listened observed, 'That drunken peasant Bonifas, may his
entrails shrink, may he die in a ditch,' (which is exactly how it
turned out in the end). Then the good people went to bed
shaking their heads at the fate which they knew would overtake
Bonifas, but making sure the shutters on their windows were
locked all the same. But not for some years did anything over-
come him. He just went on drinking two or three whole bottles
of vodka before he became drunk enough to notice. After a
while it took four or five bottles of vodka. It was about then
that Bonifas became worse in his behaviour than anyone could
remember, and not long after that, he died.

One morning it was discovered that the graveyard had been
desecrated. All the stones were knocked over, and everything
kicked and dirtied. The earth, loose from the rain which had
been falling endlessly for the past few weeks, was piled up.
When the beadle (who was also the grave-digger) Reb Sholem
Pinsk, came to the graveyard that morning to measure up a
grave for a good friend who had asked for a nice piece near
the synagogue (so that everyone could see his name) he was
amazed at the sight. He was a pious man although somewhat
short-sighted, and when he first saw the graveyard that morning he thought the dead had risen, and began to imagine he
had been chosen to announce the Messiah. But when he realized
at last what had actually happened, he ran into the village
shouting to everyone he met. He went on running until he got
to the house of the rabbi to whom he told the dreadful story.

The rabbi sat him down and gave him tea freshly poured,

E

and got him to repeat the whole story. Then the rabbi thought for a long while, pulling at his white beard, and side whiskers, for he still had all his hair although being as he was old it was snow-white. The rabbi thought and thought, and sometimes he stopped pulling his beard to ask a question, but always he was thinking. Finally he said, 'Come Reb Sholem. Let us go together to see what actually has happened.'

Everyone was already at the graveyard, and when the rabbi arrived, began at once to ask him questions. But he just stood there quietly pulling his beard, till Reb Sholem began to feel a little impatient with all this thinking and pulling white beards.

'If this had happened in Pinsk,' he grumbled, 'we should already be doing something, not standing about like a lot of old women, pulling our beards.'

He was at once silenced sternly for his lack of respect, and the rabbi was just about to make a wise observation when there was heard shouting, and down the road came running two short, sturdy, clean-shaven men wearing leather aprons. My great-grandfather remarked correctly, 'It is the two brothers Grigor and Saba from the other village, whom I know because they make my boots.'

These two brothers were, you understand, cobblers as well as Bonifas, although they didn't drink so much, and never insulted the rabbi, or stood about swearing and cursing. In spite of this they didn't get as much trade as Bonifas, simply because although they were good men they were bad bootmakers, and also because if you didn't go to Bonifas fairly often he came to you, and then there was likely to be something broken. My great-grandfather, however, had always said, 'That drunken dog will never make my boots, and if he comes shouting around here, he'll be lucky to get away with a chisel through his neck.' He always went to the brothers Grigor and Saba for his boots.

As the brothers came running up they shouted about the grave-yard, telling everyone that Bonifas had torn up the tomb-stones and dirtied everything, and straightaway they made themselves a few more clients. The rabbi pulled his beard and replied, eagerly, 'I am not surprised. This was in my mind. This Bonifas is a malignant.'

Now that they had evidence as to who had desecrated the graveyard, the rabbi said he would go and make a formal complaint to the constable. He went to get his high hat and frock-coat, first telling Reb Sholem Pinsk to clean up the graveyard, which was, after all, what he was paid for.

My great-grandfather and my young grandfather went back to breakfast, my great-grandfather complaining in his deep bass voice, 'Make a complaint to the constable! And what will the constable do? He will go and have a drink with Bonifas, that drunken impious dog Bonifas.' To which my young grandfather replied, 'Why doesn't someone simply hit Bonifas very hard?'

My great-grandfather thought this remark over, slowly rubbing his nose meanwhile. My young grandfather ran on into the house and by the time my great-grandfather arrived, three fresh rolls had already been eaten.

Although it had not rained for a few hours, it started again as my great-grandfather drank his third glass of tea. When he had finished it, he went out saying he had to go to see Grigor and Saba about a new pair of boots. Now when the father says he is going to see about a new pair of boots you mustn't question him, although you may know that new boots have only arrived two weeks ago. So my young grandfather didn't contradict, but simply thought he could play the entire morning. Which was not, as it happens, true, because at that very moment my great-grandfather decided he should crawl under the stove to clean out from the chickens and bring out the eggs if any.

As my great-grandfather had truly said, all the constable did was go to see Bonifas, get drunk with him and then stand in the rain shouting curses even worse than those normally used by Bonifas himself. My great-grandfather on hearing the accursed pair quietly prayed 'May the rain burn their lips away.' But the swearing continued, it rained more heavily than ever, and they still kept their lips. That night something happened worse even than the graveyard business.

Late that night only the rabbi was still awake, his lamp burning, studying. He sat quietly reading while outside the rain fell and a high wind blew. But the rabbi didn't hear what went on because he was studying so hard, and anyhow he had heard wind and rain often before, so why should he now after so many years start taking notice?

But suddenly there was a beating at the door and a rattling at the window. The rabbi looked up as the window was broken. Glass fell all over the room, and through the hole came stones and muck which fell mostly on the rabbi's white hair and beard. With the rubbish the wind rushed in blowing rain everywhere, and with it all a string of curses from that drunken Bonifas who had been outside swearing loudly against the wind as he watched the rabbi study quietly his holy book.

The rabbi wiped his face and called out of the window, but listening for an answer, heard only the wind whining like a devil, so very sensibly, he stuffed some rags into the broken window, cleaned up the mess and went to bed.

The next morning my great-grandfather and everyone else heard of all this, though none of them heard that Bonifas was at this moment lying with his face in a deep puddle of water near the graveyard. Later that day Reb Sholem Pinsk called round to tell them. Whereupon my great-grandfather hoped, 'Perhaps the water will put out the fire in his head.'

Several people who had to travel that road saw Bonifas lying there and also thought that a little rain would do him no harm. In the end he lay there for three days, until the rain stopped, with no one doing anything but look down their nose as they hurried past thinking Bonifas was a fool to lie in the damp for so long.

It was the constable, the friend of Bonifas, who while walking down to the village to see what he could collect in the way of presents for looking after everyone so well, found the cobbler lying in the road with the puddle deep about his head. The constable, recognizing Bonifas, laughed and called to him, then kicked and prodded him. But he didn't move. After kicking him a little more the constable pushed the cobbler over onto his back, whereupon he saw that the face of Bonifas had altered to an unusual colour and was bloated with water. The constable now realized that Bonifas was dead, and as he went into the village to announce the discovery felt like a high official. Although he would miss drinking brandy with Bonifas, he would enjoy finding someone to blame for his death.

So he went into the village and announced the death and asked questions, receiving from all the answer that Bonifas had been struck by lightning because of what he had done to the graveyard and to the rabbi. The constable sent in a report which someone wrote out for him, and everyone waited for officers to come from a town fifteen miles away. As for Bonifas, he was left on a pile of timber near the graveyard, where he lay without anyone bothering about him for four days. On the fourth day the officers arrived, including a doctor who had a very good name as a surgeon.

This doctor had earned his good name by curing some cows

of a disease which no one had even known them to be sick with. Then he was called in by the biggest land-owner in the district to look after his son who was very ill. By chance the boy lived, and this further developed the doctor's name. When he arrived with the other officers, the whole village knew about it and waited around the pile of timber where the body of Bonifas had been lying for four days. The officers walked about with the constable questioning everyone who had not given him a present lately, while the great doctor examined the body. He could see that Bonifas was dead even without listening to his heart, but he listened to make sure.

Just then my young grandfather managed to climb out of the barn where Yaacov the village teacher had locked all the boys while he went off to watch the officers. My grandfather being the smallest had been lifted up by the other boys to a narrow window in the loft of the barn, but once there found he couldn't lift anyone else up, so he got through the window himself and ran off to see what was happening to Bonifas. When he arrived the body of Bonifas had been moved onto some planks of timber, and Yaacov was busy being questioned by the other officers. This was mainly because he had never given the constable a present. Why should he? Had the constable ever given him anything? Anyway my grandfather was pleased because his teacher was too busy to notice him as he squeezed through the crowd watching the doctor listen to Bonifas' heart. The doctor concluded that Bonifas was dead because his heart had completely stopped. He adjusted his pince-nez, and it was soon after this that my grandfather had the honour of assisting at a brain operation.

When the doctor discovered it was safe, he decided to operate on Bonifas' brain, because he had never operated on a brain before, and also because there was a large bump on the head of Bonifas which seemed to be quite unusual. He got out a knife and cut round the skin, and then he got out a saw and began to saw through the bone. Everyone standing round nudged one another, saying, 'Have you ever seen such a wonderful doctor?' When the doctor sawed right through the bone, they all cheered and he turned round and bowed slightly. Then he took off the bone cup of the head of Bonifas and handed it to my grandfather who was standing right there in front. My grandfather held onto the bone cup while the doctor looked at the brain of Bonifas, in which he seemed to find nothing that interested him.

As he stood there my grandfather thought how jealous the other boys would be when they heard how he had helped the doctor. When the doctor at last took it back he wasn't sorry because it was heavy, but he was pleased so many people had seen him hold it, in case the other boys called him a liar when he told them.

Then the doctor made a dart for Bonifas' stomach. He made two long cuts in it and moved away quickly. Everyone else moved away quickly too, because at once the whole place was full of the smell of brandy and vodka and rotten food. The doctor called away the officers who were still asking questions, and told them he was ready to make his report. Then he turned to the crowd and shouted that Bonifas had died because brandy had burned his stomach away inside, and that was all there was to it. He told the officers to tell the constable to get the body buried, after which formalities everyone went away saying that Bonifas had got what he deserved.

When my grandfather arrived home he found my great-grandfather talking to Grigor and Saba. After he had told them what had happened my great-grandfather got out a bottle of brandy and poured out three glasses full. Then Grigor and

Saba shook each other by the hand. As they drank their brandy my young grandfather kept saying that brandy had burnt the stomach out of Bonifas. But my great-grandfather replied that Bonifas had died for different reasons, and they were all good, both from the religious and from the commercial points of view. And he raised his second glass of brandy to Grigor and Saba who were delighted to be the only cobblers—though clumsy ones—in the entire district.

III

Good Business With Sentiment

A LIFE IN ART

WHAT is the use of pretending? Pelk knew, even as a boy, even in the moment of exultation when the head of the art department shook him by the hand and said, 'Cooper might have painted that sheep's head,' he always knew that however right his hand might be, his temperament was wrong for a successful life in art.

For Pelk dressed sombrely and was quiet. His habits were regular, his ideas conventional. Colour, even in paintings, worried him unduly. He preferred his personality to be pale as a ghost. And while the Academy was completely discredited by violent young men whose pictures were robust with colour, Pelk painted away regularly and without excitement, working like a mathematician to make the view on the canvas precisely equal to the view he looked at.

After a few years Pelk still painted on in spite of his job with a frame-maker. He had patiently grown a moustache hoping to balance his recessive chin and large eyebrows. Strangely enough it gave his face a certain authority. People began to notice his serious unsmiling eyes and grew to respect his suggestions for framing. Several important clients always headed their instructions 'Attention Pelk'. He might have made a career as an understanding frame-maker, and he would have been satisfied. But Life will never let well alone and one day Pelk received a note on beautifully engraved note-paper asking him to call on Mr Marmourian at his famous gallery in Bond Street.

As Pelk wandered over the crimson carpet looking at the fine eighteenth-century paintings with genuine appreciation he was surprised by Marmourian himself. The great dealer had been standing just behind him for some seconds before he spoke his name.

'Pelk,' he said in his slightly throaty way, 'Pelk, is it not? The clever frame-maker who truly cares for what he frames. What is your opinion on this little Fragonard you find so intriguing?' And with that confidence of the timid when invited to speak about his soul's delight—and there is not a solitary timid soul which does not have some secret delight or other— Arthur Pelk spoke of the little painting with thought and love and clarity.

When he finished, a faint blush glowed to either side of his moustache, and Marmourian shook him by the hand and then dashed a tear from his eye as he led the way to his private office. 'It is exactly as you say,' he said. 'You have truly understood the picture. If I were a client I would have bought it— yes, yes, I could not have resisted.'

When Pelk left the Marmourian Gallery it was as a newly engaged salesman, six pounds a week plus commission, to start in a fortnight. 'You are in the greatest profession of all, my Pelk,' the dealer had said, 'for if a man paints well it is God's gift—but to sell pictures a man must really work.' Pelk was certainly frightened, but the prospect of living henceforward on intimate terms with dead and undisputed masters gave him confidence, and within three months he had married a rather nice girl whose artistic interests had never ventured beyond barbola work.

And this is really all that happened to Arthur Pelk for thirteen years. His knowledge increased—his salary grew—his commissions were substantial—his timidity was concealed by a moustache and eyebrows which were recognized in the world of art. But he remained a secret painter. And, thirteen years after his introduction to Marmourian, Arthur Pelk was distressed to realize that somewhere inside him that old juvenile desire to be a recognized artist still fluttered its imprisoned wings.

Immersed as he was in successive vogues for the various dead painters who become, every four or five years, the only fashionable masters, it was inevitable that a simple-minded craftsman like Pelk should be variously influenced. When the slight landscapes of the Frenchman Coutet were keenly sought after (Marmourian having bought a vast collection of works by this obscure little Toulouse genius well beforehand), Pelk discovered one evening that his hand and brush were automatically following out the style of Coutet. In fact, four hours produced a very passable Coutet indeed.

And so it was with Pelzner and Pieter de Wint, Gerhart Ister and Charles Bicking. Every minor master to be handled by the Marmourian Gallery became to well-understood by Pelk that his brush unfailingly emulated their strokes. He found that he was a perfect painters' medium (or possibly ghost). His first real victory, though, was when Marmourian, while taking a cocktail with the Pelks, glanced at one of Arthur's little seashore paintings and said, 'A good eye, Arthur, you have—a pretty little Boudin, I think. But to buy for yourself—is not ethical, my dear Pelk.' This chance mistake in identity at once set the vanity of the old student fluttering away like mad in Pelk's breast.

It so happened that at the time when Pelk's vanity was fluttering, collectors were becoming much interested in that charming artist Constantin Guys. After his thirteen years in the trade Pelk could easily understand the saleability of the delightful pen and wash drawings. Reasonably enough everyone suddenly wanted parasols and top hats, the freshness and immediacy of the Guys sketches, the atmosphere, the delicacy.... Pelk had no difficulty in selling at ever-increasing prices every Guys the talented Marmourian could lay his hands on. It was just as easy for him of a Sunday afternoon, inspired by some fine antique cartridge paper, to draw some of the prettiest Guys sketches Marmourian had ever seen.

No one will believe (though it is a simple fact) that Pelk had no motivation other than suppressed artistic vanity when, one dull winter morning when Bond Street was swathed in a fog to depress even Whistler, he carefully slipped seven of his Guys-style sketches into the folder reserved for that artist. Yet everyone will have to believe that Pelk acted in this way without the desire for illicit profit. For he made no false entries in the books—absolutely no money passed into his hands.

It was a quiet day and Pelk spent it in secret delight at having found his true place in a master's folder. He proposed to leave his drawings there for a few hours—perhaps even show them to an unimportant client or two, and then take them back home to the spare room where he worked. But every eye seemed to be upon him whenever he made a move to retrieve his drawings from the Guys folder. And not a single client entered the gallery that day.

Pelk hung about long after his usual time for leaving, and still it was impossible for him to retrieve his work. He planned a dozen different attempts on the folder. Each time he heard in his mind's ear the throaty voice of Marmourian, 'Caught you red-handed, my Pelk—stealing from me—your employer —your friend.' 'But they are mine,' Pelk would cry. Who would believe him? He left the drawings where they were and hurried home.

The next day Pelk found a few moments in which to take out the folder. Sure enough he heard the throaty voice of

Marmourian, introducing to him a pale gabardine-draped gentleman—'the greatest collector of Constantin Guys in America—in the World.' The American smiled and held out his hand. Marmourian patted Pelk on the back as a promoter might pat his prize heavy-weight. Palk wanted to scream and cry "I'm ill, I'm ill.' But the American was already studying the drawings in the folder.

For twenty-five minutes Pelk, his blood like liquid ice, excelled himself. He used every device in his salesmanship, every word in his vocabulary of hyperbole, every gesture of the hands, the shoulders. Persuasion, intimidation, flattery, all failed. The only drawings the American would buy were Pelk's own poor imitations. He held in delicate fingers a Guys of ten ladies in a row all with parasols—it was the best of Pelk's efforts. 'The best I have ever seen,' he said. 'I will take it, and this, and these.' And he left only one small Pelk, alone with thirty-three authentic drawings.

After Marmourian had received the cheque (and the price was really fantastic, for the pound had only recently been devalued), the great dealer turned to Pelk. 'My clever Pelk,' he said in a broken voice. 'You are the greatest of us all. These new little things—I even forget I have them—they must have cost practically nothing.' Which indeed was true. But what could Pelk do? He accepted the praise and the extra commission and went home to sit moodily cursing his vanity and his skill.

He looked about him at the well-furnished sitting-room of the new house his commissions had given him. That delightful little Louis Quinze secrétaire—it reminded him of a small Watteau, wonderfully authenticated, he had handled. That Meissen inkstand—a Corot had given him that. Art had served him well, as a loving hand-maiden serves, while he—he had betrayed her. And her consort Marmourian also he had be-trayed. For what? For a little itching vanity—the unexpired portion of his boyhood dream of fame. What was he after all these years at the elbow of greatness—A copyist. A vain, un-talented, slinking, cowardly copyist. And—my God!—a forger too. The hair on the back of Pelk's neck felt electric. The cold dead hand of horror gripped his heart.

Nothing in the range of human feeling can equal the misery of the timid man who realizes that he has destroyed the only defence his timidity has ever devised. The little bits he had prized so greatly now seemed to Pelk resentfully out of place. His own work—those quiet evenings with the brush and pen in the spare room—looked at him askance, as if the authentic works were shouting from a thousand galleries, 'How dare *you* trace *us*—perfect lines by real masters!' And night after night Pelk tossed and turned in torment as he fell through a brilliantly sketched maelstrom (rather like Leonardo's torrents) while the voices of a myriad *objets d'art* screamed 'Shame, shame'.

So it was that Pelk, his eyes dark with worry, his back bent, his hands shaking, went through the polite routine of mort-gaging his house. The bank manager gladly accepted Mr Pelk's life insurance as further collateral. Was there anything else he could arrange for Mr Pelk? There was no limit to the overdraft he might have—provided there were suitable securities. A few hundred safe Industrials—'We might as well add those. Good morning, Mr Pelk, good morning.' Such was the extreme to which Pelk was forced by artistic conscience. For he new there was no alternative. He had to buy—buy with hard money—buy back those damn' creations of his over-eager imitative hand.

So it was too that after protracted negotiations through one of Marmourian's competitors Pelk purchased back his own drawings, changed only by the addition of the impressive stamp of a famous American collection. Pelk was penniless but his peace of mind for a day or two was beyond the understanding of those mere art-dealers who lack honest feeling for authentic and original art. It was sheer bad luck that someone had to tell Marmourian that the drawings had changed hands again at an even more important price than he had obtained. And it was a tribute to Marmourian's knowledge of one of the most complicated and secretive trades ever devised by cupidity that within forty-eight hours he knew Pelk was the purchaser.

'My Pelk,' he said in sorrow. 'You underhand dog,' he cried in anger, thinking of the profit he believed Pelk was about to make. 'I take you—I make you,' he wept. 'I break you,' he screamed. 'How many times have you cheated me?' After thirteen years Pelk's integrity had completely triumphed. But he was up to his eyes in debt. And he was no longer Marmourian's star salesman.

Pelk surveyed the situation in the gloominess of the spare room that evening. His wife was busy with her barbola. He had tried to lose himself in the practice of his art, but it was useless. By some peculiar quirk of the mind he found himself in his distress painting after that unfashionable Victorian academician Cooper—a sheep's head like the one he had been so fatally complimented upon in the promising days of his youth. 'But by God,' said Pelk aloud, 'it is exactly like Cooper—a little stronger if anything.' His Guys sketches were, after all, thoroughly authenticated. And naturally every other collector in the world would hear of them and lust after them.

A man in his despair has a single moment of vision, like the panorama a drowning man is supposed to view in the moment before complete submersion. Pelk had the courage to believe in his vision. Once again his house is his, once again he is solvent, while the trade says again and again, 'You know Pelk, of course —how does he find them? Coutets, Pelzners, de Wints, Gerhart Isters, and Bickings. And Guys—of course, Pelk is the specialist in Constantin Guys.'

TOO MUCH MAN

LENNY runs this salt-beef bar, The Roll-Mop, near Windmill Street. Whenever I am round that area I drop in for lunch whatever time of day, because Lenny is a fellow who carries a good twenty stone. This makes me feel like Gary Cooper. I am also highly partial to salt-beef.

The Roll-Mop does great business because the truth about selling people food is you should look like you enjoy it yourself and want them to get the same fun out of life. This Lenny does with his big fresh fat face, in which the eyes, nose, and mouth are set with a strong delicacy as tasteful as his menu. Sometimes there are ten of us pretty fat men with a lickerish tooth for delicatessen in The Roll-Mop at the same time. But believe me, though we are packed tighter than roll-mops in a bottle we are all feeling very slim because there is good old Lenny bigger than any of us and proud of it.

'Have another lutka,' he philosophises, 'try the strudel. Take another vienna. Don't worry—how many times do you live anyway? And if it knocks five years off your life, so you will drop dead with a good flavour in your hollow tooth.' This spiel helps morale and it doesn't do business any harm either.

And that's how it was, a long, delightful gorge without conscience—till the rot set in. The rot was called Renée and she was in the front row of the show round the corner.

Of course, The Roll-Mop was headquarters for a lot of the girls from around, including many from the different theatrical productions which are such a colourful feature in the Shaftesbury Avenue vicinity. But though Lenny was prone to a laugh and a joke and maybe even a slap now and then here and there, the actual rot itself had never before set in to his slightly enlarged heart-works. Certainly—the occasional friendship, but never like this Renée performance.

I first saw Renée on a Tuesday morning about eleven when, happening to pass that way, I dropped into The Roll-Mop for an early lunch. The bar was empty except for good old Lenny talking with (and this was unusual) sad brown eyes and a serious worried expression on his usually joyous chops to this strawberry blonde, or maybe the colour her hair was dyed is called pink champagne. She stood a bit less than average height but with a more than average build on all sides and with big eyes and, it goes without saying, longer than average legs. What you might call a pocket Venus if you can afford to carry such things in your pocket.

'But why not, Renée?' Lenny was saying as I came in. 'We can have a marvellous time. It's a first-rate occasion and the eats will also be first-rate, not to mention the band, which is a specialist in South American.' He swayed his hips a little, clicking his teeth and flicking his fingers gaily.

'I can't,' said Renée, looking embarrassed at me. 'Serve the gentleman,' she continued as Lenny's face collapsed into depression. 'I have to pop now for rehearsal.'

As she popped both Lenny and I watched her.

'Seems a nice class of girl, Lenny,' I said.

'She's real class, Wolfie,' he sighed. 'What can I give you, Wolfie, the usual?'

He sliced me the usual, sighing. He sighed as he put mustard on it, and as he slipped a pickled cucumber onto the plate sighed yet again.

'Business so bad, Lenny?' I asked him.

'What's business against a happy life?' he answered.

'I thought you was married,' I replied through a mouthful of the best salt-beef in Soho.

'Me? Never,' he said, 'and it looks like I never will.'

Then, with tears in his eyes he told me. 'The truth is, Wolfie,' he said, carving off a little slice of beef and popping it into his mouth sadly, 'the truth is I embarrass her. Not me personally, but the weight—the weight is an embarrassing thing for her. I read somewhere a famous writer says inside every fat man is a thin man screaming to get free. First time in my life, Wolfie, I can hear him screaming.'

I finished my sandwich but the second half didn't have the taste—not with Lenny mooning around slipping bits of this and that into his mouth so miserably.

'Listen, Lenny,' I advised him, 'If she can't appreciate you through all that blubber, she's not worth breaking your heart over.'

'Don't tell me,' he replied, 'tell my breaking heart.'

How can you enjoy delicatessen served by a love-sick salt-beef slicer? I wasn't the only one. Within the next few weeks the Roll-Mop's business dropped off. Fat men like me just don't enjoy the disapproval of eating that radiated from Lenny like heat-waves off freshly cooked pastrami.

Also Lenny was getting the sagging look of an empty salami skin that tells you a man is murdering his gluttonous metabolism by enforced starvation. No more the big fat smile of encouragement as he cut your sandwich. As for lutkas—they were right off the menu.

'You look like you're wasting to death,' I said to him one afternoon as I chewed a late lunch more out of nostalgia than enjoyment.

'I'm down to eighteen stone,' he replied, a sad pride lighting his sallow features. 'Renée says if I take off another few stone

maybe she will reconsider things. The weight was an embarrassing thing to her.'

'You already told me,' I reminded him. 'I think you are up
the pole to throw away your business and your substance for a
doll-face who makes such demands. There is nothing in history
that says a fat man can't be a husband.'

'I am now trying the banana and milk diet,' he replied.
'Next month I go on to a vegetable-juice torture which is
guaranteed to produce startling losses. Tonight Renée has con-
sented to come to the pictures with me, so it's an occasion.
Unfortunately, it turns out, the film is with Burt Lancaster, also
a very slim man. Still, I'm making progress.'

This progress Lenny finally completed after working through
a raw potato diet, an all-meat régime, a fortnight session
devoted exclusively to acid fruit, and a five-day stint on nothing
but glucose. He was a pasty miserable fifteen stone when he told
me that he was going to close the shop for a month's holiday at
what is laughingly called a 'health hydro'.

'How's Renée?' I asked.

'Life is very difficult,' he replied, 'now she says I am not jolly
like I used to be—a thing which she always very much appreci-
ated in me. What can I do? I'm slim but I don't feel jolly.
Thank God Renée gets on with my mother. That at least is
something to be thankful for.'

'Have a nice holiday,' I replied.

Lenny told me that at that hydro they gave him the works
with massage and sun-ray and infra-red and ultra-violet and
various other rays which are hardly on the market yet. Also
with vitamins, enzymes, and gland-extracts. Also massage,
body-building, muscle development, and fresh air—not to
mention a special juice from pressed mangold-wurzels which is
the richest drink in something or other ever discovered.

'Give me the address,' I asked Lenny, because he really looked in great shape when he got back.

Now he was sad, with his hair longer and his eyes big and brown and full of thought, and his mouth rather sensitive, as if he was easily hurt. And since he was always tall with the fat off him he looked real well-built, especially since his suits didn't look like tents anymore. Even his personality had changed. He had a feeling about him like he was studying in his own mind the real meaning of life and was about to come to such a miserable answer you wanted to hug him to cheer him up. Not me, that is. I thought it was all a tragedy for the salt-beef business. But Renée, she was always in there hugging him. 'Didn't I tell him he could change himself?' she chortled.

Needless to say they got married, although I don't know which health hydro the honeymoon was spent in because frankly the whole affair disgusted me slightly. I hate to see a fellow's nature put upon by a pocket Venus of whatever size. There are other salt-beef bars in Soho, so I went to them. But it wasn't like The Roll-Mop used to be.

One lunch-time I was in the vicinity of Lenny's place, so I thought for old-time's sake—why not? I looked in. I say look —but it was more like a squint, the place was so packed with fat men all knocking back salt-beef sandwiches by the gross. Surprised, I pushed my way through to the bar.

'Wolfie,' greeted Lenny as he handed plates past a buxom pretty brunette who looked after the cash-register. 'Where you been? The usual? Go on—enjoy yourself. How long have you got to live, anyway?'

'You put on weight, Lenny,' I said, because there he was back with more or less the same twenty stone he had before the rot set in.

'Listen,' he said, 'is it a better thing to be a bit on the plump side and contented or to have a figure and cry like Johnnie Ray the whole time?'

'Johnnie Ray?' said the buxom brunette, 'I'll say. With that miserable look he couldn't keep the girls away.' She punched the cash-register steadily as she talked. 'But a couple of months' real eating got him back to normal,' she continued smugly.

'She took me to every delicatessen in town. And eat—I had to eat my best to keep up with her,' added Lenny. 'You know my wife Renée of course.' He introduced me to the brunette.

'Didn't you used to be blonde?' I asked.

She shook her dark curls. Already she was getting the dew-lapped look of the constant eater-between-meals.

'Blonde is not really suitable for the eating business,' she explained. 'Lenny, dolly, you want more butter on your baigel?'

'You see,' Lenny explained out of the side of his full mouth, 'now we are married the weight is no longer embarrassing to her.' He patted his enormous stomach. 'What do we always say, Renée?' he asked.

She stretched out her hand and also patted. 'What we always say is,' she said, 'if you got the right man, how can you have too much?'

LA VIE EN ROSE

'JEAN-LOUIS is an efficiency expert, really, aren't you, Jean-Louis, an efficiency expert?' The dark girl with short legs like pea-nuts wriggled in her armchair.

Mrs Pargeter, the grocer's wife, looked at Jean-Louis and thought how expensive all those fancy French cheeses were. But they bought them, so what could you say? A good bit of cheddar took some beating though, say what you like, you can't beat the old cheddar when it's good. Half the time you couldn't make out what they were saying. It must be terrible to be a foreigner.

'Yes?' said Mr Pargeter, wiping his moustache gently with a dark-blue handkerchief. 'Must be interesting work. Take the grocery for instance. In the grocery you have to be efficient, I don't care what you say, take any perishable goods for instance, if you order too many of them and you have miscalculated your public, why then, what's the net result? Loss, sheer gross loss.'

'Please,' said Jean-Louis, 'a little more quick. I am in England four months. If you go a little more quick I am listen and do understand how you are speak.'

'A little slower, Jean-Louis,' the dark girl said. 'His English is wonderful considering. I think he has done wonders considering.'

She showed her teeth to Jean-Louis and wriggled again. He smiled winningly at Mrs Pargeter. The grocer's wife smiled back thinking I'm not sorry that Dorothy left the shop when she did. Women with big teeth are always a bit that way although I don't say she wasn't a good cashier.

Mr Pargeter was watching the dark girl cross her legs. Short but sturdy, he thought, these girls with strong legs take some beating say what you like. He laughed.

'Let us all share in your little joke, Fred,' said Mrs Pargeter with *that* smile. If she caught him pinching the Ramage girl's bottom again underneath the counter *she* would have a go too. 'It's not fair to keep a good joke to oneself, is it, Mr Payray?' Mind you, foreigners had nice smiles and a brown shirt with a brown tie to match gave them an air of you-know.

'Call him Jean-Louis, Mrs Pargeter,' said the dark girl. 'In Paree one does not stand on ceremony, n'est ce pas, Jean-Louis?'

'Pé-ré, P, EY, R, EY, Pé-ré,' explained Jean-Louis.

'Pay-ray, Pay-ray,' answered Mrs Pargeter, 'I've got it.'

'Ta-ra-ra-boom-de-ay,' said Mr Pargeter.

'Just call him Jean-Louis, he won't mind.' The dark girl uncrossed her legs.

The marines was there, thought Mr Pargeter.

'How about another drink? Drink, Mr uh-pay——'

'Pay-ray, Fred. Fred has no grasp I'm afraid, though he's a wonder on figures.' Mrs Pargeter's temper was fraying a little.

Ay-ay, thought Mr Pargeter as Jean-Louis crossed to the dark girl's chair and edged his arm round her waist. You can't beat it, Mr Pargeter thought.

'Now what are we all drinking?'

'Plain Vermouth for Jean-Louis, isn't it darling, just the Vermouth plain?'

'I think you've had enough, Fred,' Mrs Pargeter said with that smile again. But Mr Pargeter was asking the dark girl how she liked it, long or with less water than gin, take your choice. Pretending he didn't notice his wife's warning, he poured himself another large whisky.

'Well, here's all the best to all of us, and may we all get whatever we want in life.' He drank half the whisky in the glass. 'Good luck to us all,' he said, 'best of luck Mr What-not, good luck, Dorothy, don't do anything I wouldn't do, all the best dear. Drink up.'

They drank up, Mrs Pargeter giving Mr Pargeter the signal to slow down, Jean-Louis looking deep into the dark girl's eyes which tried to look back over the rim of the glass. His hand was on the dark girl's thigh. Mr Pargeter caught the signal, and refilled his glass quickly.

'One last one for the road, my dear,' he said, 'last one, longest one. That's the ticket John-Louey,' he added as Jean-Louis pushed the dark girl's glass away and kissed her full on the mouth.

'Well,' Mrs Pargeter said, 'well, there is a limit.' This is the last time that hussy comes into my house with her fancy men, and Fred looking at them as if they were a couple of rabbits, well, after all, well.

'Fred,' she said sternly, 'what's the time, Fred? It must be after eleven.' She managed to get that smile into her voice, and it brought the dark girl to her senses.

'Look at us,' she giggled. 'Really, Jean-Louis, this isn't Gay Paree, you have to watch your p's and q's. I say, what a fright I must be looking. Oh, dear, Mr and Mrs P, whatever will you be thinking of us? I don't know what I shall look like in the morning.'

Jean-Louis was bumbling into her ear:

> *When I took you in my arm*
> *Je vois la vie en rose.*

She pushed his hand away and stretched for her bag. Mr Pargeter smiled as he reached absent-mindedly for the bottle. But

Mrs Pargeter reached it first and tucked it firmly under her chair.

The dark girl used a thin lipstick quickly, giving herself a neat outline which ignored her lips completely.

'I don't know how I shall look in the morning. I'm terrible getting up in the morning.'

Mr Pargeter leered over her compact mirror.

'It's nicer to lie in bed, Dorothy love,' he said.

They watched Jean-Louis accompany his song with a few neat dance-steps.

'He's always like that,' the dark girl said proudly, 'soon as he wakes up, bounces out of bed, full of beans.'

'Well!' Mrs Pargeter said. 'Well!'

'So he says anyway, don't you, Jean-Louis?' the dark girl added blushing. 'Up with the lark he says,' she continued, looking away from Mrs Pargeter but with a sly grin.

'Early to bed early to rise,' said Mr Pargeter watching the dark girl's legs as she stood up.

'Good night then,' she added, 'thanks for a lovely time. Come on, Jean-Louis, maintenant bonne nuit.'

'What about one for the road?' asked Mr Pargeter.

'Now you didn't have a hat did you, dear?' Mrs Pargeter stated firmly as she coldly handed them their coats.

While she saw them to the door Mr Pargeter had the presence of mind to get the bottle from underneath the chair and pour himself a stiff one. When the front door had clicked to she came back into the room. She didn't have that smile on her face.

'I didn't invent sex you know, Emily,' he said, half-truculent, half-querulous.

But Mrs Pargeter new better.

NATURE'S WAY

THE VILLAGE in question creeps up a hill. This it has been doing for a long time but not yet long enough for the vicar's pamphlet *Crawlingtree: an historical retrospect* (privately printed in 1902) to have gone into a second impression.

Those afflicted with a sufficiently undiscriminating love of landscape may savour the quality of the Essex countryside from the brow of Crawlingtree Hill. And on this very brow they may further indulge their aestheticism by mounting to the roof of the combined shop and living accommodation of J. Scully, the local pharmacist. From this vantage point they will see scrub pasture declining towards a marshy pond, and let out to a local farmer at five pounds per annum, payable in advance. A small herd of cows of mixed origin browses disconsolately day after day upon the dry grass, or wades hopelessly knee-deep into the mud which surrounds the dark patch of water. Whether a cow has ever managed to get beyond the mud and savour two or three stomachs-full of that dingy liquor, seems, on the face of things unlikely. So that the whole herd might be expected to perish eventually from the combined effects of drought and starvation. But so persistent is the grasp upon life that apart from becoming bonier and bonier, the herd browses on. No one notices if it is ever milked. The farmer appears to have forgotten the whole matter. Presumably he feels it worth five pounds yearly in advance to get rid of the miserable creatures. Perhaps he has always wanted to be an arable farmer anyway. Whatever the case, the whole herd is painted in water-colour (well after Constable) several times a year by the older girls of a local private academy, the least talented of whom is the red-headed daughter of J. Scully, local pharmacist. J. Scully's only other distinguishing characteristic is an obsession with regularity—a condition he has consistently achieved and maintained, skilled pharmacist that he is, by nightly potations of that common but unparalleled herb, Senna—which comes, as all know—in pods.

Such the landscape against which the saga of Safelax is set. And what countryside in the world could possibly be more constipated?

Now Mrs J. Scully was a quiet efficient woman, a sleeping partner of her husband's in a very uneventful business, for Jim never quite matched his pre-marital ardour, and the Scully daughter remained the sole legatee to his home and its view.

But quiet woman as she was Mrs Scully had her demon. It drove her towards perfecting bread-pudding (use up the stale loaf) beef broth (use up the bones) paper spills (save vestas) and similar virtuous economies. She never varied in her weekly household budget of forty-five shillings. 'You can spend a little more from time to time if you like, my love,' said Jim Scully occasionally. 'You run your shop Jim,' answered his wife, 'and let me look after the house.' He took it kindly and grew to enjoy the weekly bread-pudding and regular beef broth.

It took only a very few years for Mrs Scully to effect every possible economy in the management of her simple household. Her demon felt its honour to be satisfied. She was certain that there was no wastage anywhere, and yet she felt something more could be done. Between her household motions she would stop and purse her brow and press her lips together for a moment, only to dismiss her anxiety with a shrug and turn with familiar pleasure to the mincer. But one night as she lay in their vast bed watching Jim pour hot water upon the Senna Pods in the bowl on the pot-cupboard, her eyes lit up and she sat bolt upright exclaiming. Jim turned with a pained expression on his face towards her, upset at the disturbance at a time when the least jolt to his arm might ruin the potation with too much water. 'My love,' he said, 'is something wrong? I'm rather busy you know.' 'Don't bother yourself dear,' replied Mrs Scully. She smiled quietly and was quickly asleep.

The nearest Jim Scully ever came to losing his temper with his wife followed upon this strange nocturnal behaviour of hers. He had been unusually busy the following day, for it was a dank November, and tubes were threatening to clog in the chests of the local inhabitants. Scully had a dozen times been disturbed in his reading, but he had supplied vapour rub and cough tonic with good feeling, and he had not noticed his wife's unusual trips into the shop from the adjoining parlour. It was when he had closed the shop for tea, and had actually sat down to a plate of pork sausage and mashed potato that he raised his head and sniffed deeply once or twice. Above the savoury scent of the pork he smelt the familiar odour which presaged, for him, secure sleep. The house was redolent with the scent of Senna Pods. Startled out of his customary calm, Scully leapt to his feet and ran to the kitchen.

There stood Mrs Scully in a cloud of aromatic steam, pouring an enormous black kettle of boiling water over at least six pounds of Senna Pods, a huge brown pile like autumn leaves in an enamel bowl. 'Upon my soul!' exclaimed Scully, 'what in the devil's name are you doing my love?' But Mrs Scully poured on till the kettle was empty. Then she turned to him as he stood there fuming at her inhuman behaviour to man's unswerving friend. 'I'm troubled by the waste that goes on here, Jim Scully, night after night, with you taking fresh pods for your draught. Now I shall bottle this lot and you shall have a glass every morning and you'll see how we shall save in the long run.' What use was it for Jim to try to explain that a great deal of his satisfaction lay in dropping a handful of pods in the bowl, boiling the water and pouring it carefully, night after night? What sense would the poetry of that make to a reasonable woman? He choked back his indignation and went into the shop to read leaving his tea untouched upon the table. Mrs Scully scooped up the plate and slipped it into the oven. Then she set about bottling the liquor she had brewed in so crudely wholesale a manner.

Needless to say Jim Scully eventually felt hungry and returned sheepishly to eat his tea. There is not a married man who has failed to capitulate in similar circumstances, for no sooner does anger pass than appetite returns. And when he saw all the demijohns of translucent brown liquid lined up on a shelf he did feel, to tell the truth, a sort of satisfaction. He tried to calculate how long his supply would last. He wondered at the vast period of regularity those bottles represented. And although he poured his morrow's draught with a certain amount of trepidation and a definite sense of loss, he was delighted in the morning to discover that the liquor had lost none of its potency in its new economic form.

It so happened that Scully's neighbour, a baker who supplied the entire village and district with bread, had a piece of rather bad luck at almost the very moment that Mrs Scully was pouring her large black kettle. This baker—his name is of no importance for in spite of the part he has unwittingly played in all our lives we shall not refer to him again—this baker then, had, for private reasons, agreed to do a friend a turn, and store six sacks of plaster of paris for him. The baker, as a matter of fact, had been proposing to whitewash his bakery for some time and a little plaster out of each sack would hardly be noticed. It would probably do the job very well, and anyhow, he wasn't charging the man rent. But so secretive did his plan make him that he completely forgot to mention the presence of the sacks to his assistant. By the time the baker himself came down to supervise that night's baking, two complete sacks of plaster had been converted into bread. Fortunately they had mixed in well with the flour and apart from the loaves being a little heavier than usual, no difference was noticeable. 'A little plaster's not going to do them any harm—and as for him, he'll just have to take his loss in bad part if he feels that way,' the baker philosophically observed to his apprentice. He was gratified to hear several of his customers comment on how white the bread was. 'It certainly won't poison them—that's flat,' he remarked to his wife. 'All's well that ends well.'

The baker's error may perhaps be considered an example of the way trade circulates and creates trade. Within twenty-four hours Jim Scully was being disturbed in his reading by customer after customer demanding 'something safe'. His remaining supply of Senna Pods was exhausted very soon—and still they came. One after another the demijohns were taken down, and ounce by liquid ounce they were emptied. Furthermore the customers were delighted to find that they could take the draught without waiting, without bothering to potate it themselves. Their urgency was great and they were thankful. Neither they nor Scully realized until the entire stock was cleared that, liquid ounces being somewhat heavier than the dry herbs, the firm of J. Scully had cleared a little over four hundred per cent profit on its entire stock of Senna Pods.

'Dear me,' said Scully when he realized what had happened, 'what shall I do, my dear?' And then, with one of those swift, transient flashes of sheer feminine insight Mrs Scully put her

F

husband on the road to fortune. 'Make some more of course. Make some more.' And already she had the kettle on while she bundled Scully onto his bicycle and sent him off to the next village to buy up the local pharmacist's stock of Senna.

Once a human soul accidentally slips onto its right road, nothing can stop its growth. Most souls can only peep out once or twice before freeing themselves of the wearisome burden of the flesh, and yearn wistfully after their destiny. But let ambition and circumstance meet but once. The quietest soul will swell to gigantic proportions.

Thus it was that while Jim Scully preserved, though always now with some small irritable frustration, his regularity, and a smart young man encouraged the growing demands in the shop, Mrs Scully brought the principles of household economy to bear upon what had started as pure inspiration.

Scully's fame spread quickly among the villages. It was exciting to think of a new cure being discovered in their midst by one of their own people. It seemed old-fashioned not to try it, and conservative to wait until it was merely necessary. A little peppermint oil was added. 'It tastes so clean,' said the customers. A little bromide. 'And I sleep so well,' they told one another. Night after night in the scattered hamlets men toasted their wives in it, whilst the enthusiasm of the ladies caused a serious drop in the local sales of invalid port. But man and wife slept secure knowing that the future's mornings would always, at the very least, start well.

As for the magical name itself, Jim Scully hit upon it as he served his first customer. 'But what is it?' asked a careful lady who wasn't going to throw another bad pain after the first. 'It's safe, madam. Take my word for it,' replied Jim with habitual sincerity. 'It's new, but it's natural. It's a safe laxative. It's Safelax, that's what it is.'

We may hardly add how necessary it is to beware of imitations, and assure the reader that,

> SAFELAX, 'Nature's Way' to health
> and regularity, may be had ONLY of
> J. Scully, Crawlingtree, Essex, one
> shilling the large bottle.

THIRTY-FIVE MINUTES FROM
NOWHERE

A MAN called Woodrough woke at 6.55 on a hot summer morning surprised to find that his face was smooth with perspiration. It was light outside and the birds were chattering loudly into a day for them already well advanced. But Woodrough habitually awoke at 7.30, a habit which ensured—what with bathing, shaving, and dressing, and drinking one cup of tea only—his appearance on the broad pavement of Piccadilly precisely fifteen minutes after his assistant was due at the office in St James's.

Woodrough was, therefore, on the particular day in question, thirty-five minutes in advance of himself.

Now Woodrough was a man to whom minutes spoke with the voice of all Time. For the adult years of his life Woodrough had been one of Time's virtuosos—a connoisseur, a collector, a dealer-doyen.

He accepted his position as only a third-generation dealer could, and he valued minutes in full appreciation of the fact that antiquity is a mere matter of time.

So that when Woodrough saw that he was thirty-five minutes to the good he at once applied himself to the problem of profiting from this unexpected advantage. He drank his tea and glanced at the paper, missing his wife's presence at the breakfast table.

Then walking out into the sunlight he was conscious of a slight feeling of discomfort—to call it danger would be to overstress Woodrough's feeling. It was simply that thirty-five minutes from nowhere are a temptation and an inconvenience as well as an asset.

Woodrough walked along Piccadilly with his usual uncon-
scious assurance, only a little put out at not encountering the
familiar nods from familiar faces.

He walked up to his office and was surprised to find the door
unlocked. 'Good Lord!' he said.

And then: 'Good Lord, Symes. What are you doing here so
early?' Woodrough's assistant had looked up from the books
spread out before him on the desk, and his face was a shocking
mask of malevolence and fear. He glanced at his watch and
looked back at Woodrough. 'My God!' he said with a break
in his voice, 'You're early!'

Woodrough's system took the shock of Symes' consistent
dishonesty with unexpected resilience. Yet a sort of dullness
behind his quiet phoning of the police betokened irremediable
loss of confidence, of trust, of money, of trade secrets. Symes
had never seemed very concerned over his selling commissions
and the memory of this too made Woodrough sad.

Afterwards Woodrough dropped in his chair behind the
desk. His mind was still fussing over the thirty-five minutes
he had saved and still not entirely consumed.

Not unnaturally, a business man in his trouble turns to a
woman. And not surprisingly, that woman is his mistress rather
than his wife—for a mistress is a better investment for sym-
pathy. Woodrough's Rose was sympathetically thornless.
Towards her his spirit bore him, away, a four-shilling taxi-ride
away to Knightsbridge, at the opposite pole to business.

Woodrough felt tired as he fished out the key and slipped
it into the lock. The door floated open silently on to the little
hall of the flat and he walked in. It was quiet and sheltered
from the sun and cool with the faintest touch of Chanel (which
for Woodrough remained timelessly fashionable), and he stood
quietly for a moment or two before turning into the bedroom.

But alas for the man of habit who tries to make thirty-five minutes on twenty-four hours! The cause of fresh bitterness snored beside Rose, his mouth open, and his face completely relaxed. She had failed Woodrough and it was more painful than Symes' betrayal.

For men who deal always in things of beauty know well how love ranks above art in price.

Woodrough turned away without a word while the strangers to his stricken heart slept on as if he were a ghost.

Then Woodrough in his misery walked fast towards St James's, and as he walked he raged and through his mind the words of resolution turned again and again. 'I will make more money—more money than Symes could steal. I will find another and another mistress, kinder than Rose and more faithful.' Rose, O Rose, he thought. And he arrived at Christie's Auction Rooms in time for a most important sale of porcelain.

Without a glance at the red and sallow faces of his fellow dealers, Woodrough walked towards the table, the crowd clearing for him with that kind of awe which primitive men reserve for the possessed. And possessed Woodrough seemed to be, as against his friends, against reason, against the great Ring itself, he bid again and again in tens of guineas for lot after lot.

The auctioneer called out his name as the hammer fell. 'Woodrough—Woodrough—Woodrough.' They looked on him, those careful valuers for probate, with the mixed horror and envy which only the potency of really great dealers can challenge.

When it was over Woodrough left the rooms unaware of the thousands he had bid away for the Meissen birds and Wedgwood vases, the Chelsea birds, and the lot of mixed items belonging to an almost bankrupt dealer who was delighted to see them fetch so inflated a price.

Woodrough, exhausted, took a taxi home. Through his mind echoed the cry 'Woodrough—Woodrough—Woodrough', though the auctioneer's voice was charged with uncustomary sorrow. There were tears in his eyes as he listened. But he felt the relief of bidding away a vast burden of agony.

Yet for all that he suffered Woodrough had still something to be grateful for. By the time the taxi reached his house and he had stumbled through the door he was too sick to notice his wife's hurried handling of the telephone.

She had found herself that day some half-hour to the good and was informing a very old family friend of their unexpected opportunity. What she felt about his early homecoming Woodrough would never appreciate. He retired to bed with the strength of his secure family life to succour him through a bout of serious blood-pressure—which is, among dealers in *objets*, almost an occupational disease.

A HANDFUL OF EARTH

MOISHE he was called, and because no one had ever thought to ask what his surname was, and because he had been selling second-hand records almost from before the invention of the gramophone, Moishe Music. His stall was in one of those short dead-end streets which lead off from Petticoat Lane like forgotten backwaters in a Venice in which the Grand Canal is two hundred thousand people sluggishly flowing between banks of bargains.

As you edged your way nearer to Moishe Music past the crated ducks cackling, the fish being gutted, the smoked salmon being sliced, and bare arms dipping into barrels for herrings and cucumbers, you'd hear Chaliapin booming through the cracked horn of an old gramophone, or Gigli, his voice just a little too high and a little too fast, chirping like a canary from behind a pile of red and green water-melons.

There was nothing on Moishe's stall later than Flanagan and Allen singing 'Underneath the Arches'. In other parts of the market you could bop and swing and jazz it anyway you liked from big loud Tannoys. But here you had to stand close to hear Nellie Melba singing 'Coming through the Rye'. There they were in boxes, Jack Hylton and his Metrognomes in quiet partnership with Carroll Gibbons, both at sixpence, and old red label classics marked down to a shilling a piece and looking like derelict hansom cabs.

Moishe was the dustman of music and I owe an astonishing knowledge of extinct music-hall numbers to his salvage work.

I used to stand among the collectors flicking over the old discs while Moishe plugged his best-seller for the week on the hand-wound gramophone—'The Song of the Flea' it might be, or 'Softly Awakes my Heart'. Slowly, carefully, considering all faults, the customers paid over their shillings and sixpences and Moishe stroked his grey-streaked beard as he slipped the coins carefully into an old-fashioned public-house till.

One Sunday Moishe was stalling-in while I still thumbed my way through a batch of early Carusos, 'Take the lot at a shilling each,' he said, 'it'll be one last bargain for you. There must be twenty-five there—here, give me a pound for the lot.'

Caruso never sang so cheap and who could resist—even if it meant stumbling home from the Underground like an overloaded camel.

'Next Sunday you won't see me here,' Moishe said as he made a parcel of the records.

'Moving to a new pitch?' I asked, thinking the parcel will weigh a ton, and what do I want so much Caruso for anyway?

Moishe handed the Caruso glut to me. It weighed a ton and a half to be precise, and the second-hand string would never last out. Then Moishe fiddled inside his shirt bringing out a small, worn, purple velvet bag.

'For fifty years I carried this round my neck. From Russia. Through Poland—sometimes I didn't have luggage, but this bag I always had. And always, right from a boy, I swore I would take it back where it belongs. To Beth Zion.'

What can a man carry around with him the best part of his life, in a small, worn velvet bag?

'Earth,' Moishe told me, 'a handful of earth from the Holy Land. Now at last I saved enough to take it back—exactly back to exactly where it come from.'

Two or three weeks afterwards habit took me against the Petticoat Lane crowd towards Moishe Music's dead-end. When no reedy ghost voice crept above the water-melons, I remembered that he had emigrated for the last time in his life. I was sorry to see him go but at the same time glad to have lost the bad habit of carrying home heavy parcels of old scratched wax.

One Sunday, when we were expecting for supper half a dozen elderly relatives who wouldn't be satisfied with anything less than the best herrings, I took the long creep to the best herring-stall in the East End—the only other feature of interest by that dead-end from where Moishe Music had emigrated. But as I trimmed my way through towards the barrels I had completely forgotten the difference between salt herrings without and with Melba.

Then, as an old brown woman with a black scarf round her head sliced the herrings with a quick snaky knife, a Russian bass started to boom out 'The Death of Boris'. I took my slightly leaking bag of herrings and pushed through towards it. Moishe was back in the music business.

There they were, the same half-dozen careful collectors sorting over the same tattered stock, while Moishe wound the same cracked gramophone.

'Did you put the earth back?' I asked.

'It's you?' Moishe shook my hand. 'I certainly did,' he explained, 'and don't think it was an easy affair. When I got to Beth Zion the whole place was covered with concrete for a dam or something they're building there.'

'So you put the earth back somewhere else?' I suggested.

'If you think,' he replied, 'that I am carrying around with me for fifty years a handful of earth from Beth Zion and I am saving and saving only to take back that handful of earth to Beth Zion, and when eventually I get to Beth Zion I am going to put that handful of earth somewhere else, then, let me tell you,' he told me, 'you are making a big mistake.'

Instead Moishe Music had given everyone a headache with

his handful of earth. He nagged so many officials that eventually they decided the quickest thing was to drill through the concrete at Beth Zion and let Moishe put the earth back. Then maybe they could get on building dams without interruption.

'Why didn't you stay, Moishe? Retire there—no?' I asked him.

'No,' he explained, 'the weather was marvellous the whole time, you can pick oranges in the garden, there's a few little political problems, but who cares about politics so long as we get Jerusalem in the end. And it's a marvellous country—but it's a country for young men to live in, not for old men like me to die in. Also, I don't mean this as a criticism, but you know what I mean when I say, well—it's marvellous there, but it's not the East End.'

He put another record on the gramophone. Then as an Italian tenor started to tra-la-la-la his way through 'The Barber of Seville', the bit every tenor always sings, Moishe fiddled under his shirt for a moment, and pulled out a new velvet bag.

'Earth,' he explained, 'from the Holy Land. I couldn't leave without a souvenir.'

FIVE PER CENT OF PARADISE

It's my luck I should be in Badarabad with a large quantity of slightly soiled Union Jacks and assorted flags of the Empire in all sizes the week they get their independence. I also have with me a few other short lines, the St George toast-rack which takes four pieces of toast secured by the ridges along the dragon's back; a nice range of tartan tea-cosies all clans; ten gross little camera with a little battery inside you press the button a light comes up and against it the fifteen most beautiful models are revealed, and a few boxes of latex hula-hula girls moving most realistically when you turn the handle underneath. But the flags are the big hope of Badarabad Trading Company. I come from a long line of small capital big hopers, some of whom have not died bankrupt.

When I arrive there Badarabad is just a small place quietly stinking in the sun with a governor and a governor's palace as magnificent as the Blue Dance Hall in the Edgware Road. The governor has got a nice old girl who is his missus, a Lady Duckworth, spends her whole time running round a ruined temple stands just by where the jungle starts, looking at what is carved on the stones. In fact the great tragedy within a couple of days of my arrival is that she has just got a few boys to pull out a stone and what is carved on it gives her such a fright she falls over in a dead faint, and the boys knock off for their rice-pudding elevenses and when they get back the old girl is completely eaten by a tiger. Sir Duckworth is pretty fed up when he hears this after he comes back from the club where he has been knocking back a few drinks at my expense. And I am pretty worried myself in case, with my luck, he should reckon it against me especially as I am taking up a lot of his time with looking at the fifteen models just once more old chap, and working one of the hula-hula girls till she falls to pieces. Still I gave him a couple more and went back to the tin hut and painted up on the board over the door 'By appointment'. Which was my second big mistake, the first being ever to come to a fly-ridden, rat-infested, dung-heap in a hot-house like Badarabad. Because it was the very next day they got their independence.

Mind you the Badarabadis don't know nothing about this independence business. Posters is being stuck up everywhere in English and Badarabadi but it is all so long and involved the rumour gets round that the British are going to land six regiments of guards and round up all the sacred goats in the place because England is short of meat. The next thing is the streets are full of screaming Badarabadis and Sir Duckworth is taken off in a destroyer with his three AD Cs and the two latex hula-hula girls, and a lot of valuable property is burnt down and looted and suddenly I am the only British resident left because I have the sense to dark my face with some brown boot-polish and put on a white overall and stand by the shop door shouting and pointing this way and that way while I jump up and down on the flag of the German Republic (what do the Badarabadis know).

And this is where I have my first piece of luck. A whole crowd of Badarabadis comes running past in a hurry since they have just looted the bank. They stop and look at me jumping on the flag and the leader asks me to step aside and has a few jumps himself. Then they all want to, and by the end of the day the fashion has spread like wild-fire and my whole stock of flags is sold at a good margin of profit. All of which is to explain how I happen to have twenty thou just handy when his Supreme

Highness, the Son of the Morning Star, the Sultan of Badarabad, decided (being as it is the end of the racing season anyway)
to visit his home town.

Now this Sultan always has a soothing effect on his people on
the rare occasions he shows up in Badarabad, sometimes after
a bad run of luck on the horses or because there are no good
musicals on in London, or maybe because Paris doesn't happen
to be in the spring just now and who wants Paris in the winter?
His Supreme Highness is only a small-time son of the Morning
Star, but as such his perks are very nice indeed. Every year
they make him a present of twenty-eight fresh girls and the
entire crop of dates. That's how much they love the dear old
Sult. But all the wherewithal for spieling in the casinos of
Monte Carlo, Las Vegas and Blackpool comes not from the
two bob's-worth of dates, or even from selling the girls, but
from being not only a sultan but a high priest. This is how the
business works, and you must admit it is rather a sweet racket,
and makes you think that the business men of the West can
learn a thing or two from the mysterious East.

The true reason why the Sultan has come back is because as
High Priest of Badarabad he had a duty to perform. This duty
consists of selling through his heavenly land-office parcels of
land in different parts of Paradise to all his trusting serfs. They
are coming once a year from far and near to put down a deposit
on a nice bit of acreage, or maybe if they are flush, buying out-
right a beautiful allotment where the crops blossom daily in
complete contrast to this stony old Badarabad dump where a
handful of rice is a day's pay. And his agents are selling from
a large map parcels at all prices, high for a good position
ranging to however much a coolie happens to have for not such
a good place down low on the map. But they are perfectly fair
about this. If the bloke comes back in a couple of years, or wants

to make a hire-purchase arrangement, they will consider the sum down a deposit, and who knows, maybe by the time the fellow actually dies he will have the best position in all Paradise. And all the proceeds (less moderate running costs) are the personal and private income of the Sultan himself. See?

Now the Sultan had returned a little early because of an unprecedented run of bad luck at twenty-one, poker, snakes and ladders and other gambling games, and he needs a few thousand on account, otherwise how will it look at Monte Carlo when he isn't the heaviest loser? The name of Badarabad will not be respected and they are a proud people. But the fact remains, they tell the Sultan, Badarabad has just had the worst crop in even its history, and the citizens are restive for this very reason, although by the time the Sultan docks and is carried on the bare backs of the multitude to his palace which is as magnificent as the Paramount Dance Hall, Tottenham Court Road, most serfs are quiet again and looking forward to market-gardening in Paradise. Still, the Sultan's agent explains, they haven't been buying too well lately, and there is only a few miserable hundred in the exchequer. Also the bank they robbed was the Sultan's personal bank, and his reserve fund is entirely blued. This is where I come in.

I call on the Sultan and offer him my whole twenty thou (what is the Badarabadi pound worth anyway?) in exchange for Hell, the complete concession, lock, stock and barrel, with a deed of ownership, sealed, signed and delivered, complete with map and all.

'You want to buy Hell?' he says. 'Can he buy Hell?' he asks his agents.

'With pleasure,' they say, 'who in their right mind would buy Hell?'

So I leave the Sultan's land office the sole owner of Hell, and in the opinion of all and sundry the biggest bloody fool between Arabia Deserta and Seven Dials.

Then with the assistance of my clerk, Jimmy, a Badarabadi who wants to become a company director one day, I draw out a handbill and we get ten thousand distributed all over the state. SPEND ETERNITY IN BADARABAD says the heading on the bill.

> All those who can't afford a pitch in Paradise needn't think they have a hope of going to Hell once dead.
>
> HELL IS COMPLETELY SOLD OUT
> Paradise is getting crammed to capacity. Speak to His Supreme Highness now about it, or look forward to spending
> ETERNITY IN BADARABAD.

The idea is horrifying to all Badarabadis. The first result is a run on the Sultan's land office so that all plots shown on the map are taken up at luxury prices. The Sultan and his agents are delighted, but there is no time to set up new maps, so in a few days the land-office and palace are besieged by Badarabadi hordes all demanding the Sultan should free them from the threat of spending eternity in Badarabad—than which even the prospect of Hell is more cheerful.

Need I say more? The Sultan comes, crown in hand to me, and I am kind enough to sell him Hell back, lock, stock and barrel, for a nominal thirty per cent profit (he always strikes a tough bargain, the old boy) plus a five per cent royalty in perpetuity on Paradise (because when it comes to making a bargain I also know a thing or two, believe me).

So you are now talking to a man who owns five per cent of Paradise and has had the great honour to have been appointed ADC to His Supreme Highness the Sultan of Badarabad, my partner and a gentleman if ever I met one.

GOOD BUSINESS WITH SENTIMENT

NATURALLY Mrs Adamson was excited about the forthcoming marriage of her daughter Elizabeth. She was excited as only an artist can be—one who has planned and worked and sighed and now sees the promised end. Or a constructional engineer who has just seen the last rivet in a fine bridge plugged home. Or a house-agent who as completed a sale. And yet how can any of these compare with the supreme satisfaction of a mother who has piloted her only daughter into a good match?

A good match it was. Elizabeth, only daughter, to Vincent, only son—and though titles are nice, capital has its importance. The whole world knew how well-capitalized Vincent's father was. And how well they looked together. Mrs Adamson's eyes filled with joyful tears as she watched her little girl crook her finger delicately.

Ah, that finger. That—to Vincent's astonished sense—that digit scented beyond the musk of exotic dreams, that little, little finger, that dream, that jewel. Elizabeth is altogether a gem not to be priced by a keen eye trained in valuation. She is rare and costly and beautifully polished—like the diamond which glistens brilliantly against her fresh pink skin.

As the day approaches, Mr Adamson takes an occasional afternoon off from the office. He sits at home by his desk carefully working over the figures for the cost of the wedding. Because he has carefully built up his family's security these twenty years past it is a reflex for him to check and double-check. On the wedding, of course, he cannot possibly show a profit. But with luck he will come through without impairing his standard of living. And Mrs Adamson will be satisfied. Above all she will be content. He sighs as he checks the figures yet again.

Fortunately he has been able to help Vincent in the matter of the ring through a very dear friend in the trade. Not a bad ring, he thinks, for the money. He smiles. As he draws the smoke into his lungs he makes a lightning calculation of the money he has spent in the past twenty years on tobacco.

On such an afternoon Mrs Adamson's excited girlish face gives in for a moment. Her expression fades, her neck wrinkles, there is an uneven dab of powder on her nose. She sighs and leaves the room to loosen her corset and snatch half-an-hour's rest before the children arrive for dinner and a discussion of the arrangement of cars. When you get to the outer fringes of large families it becomes difficult to know who is entitled to a car.

Oh, dear, whispers Mrs Adamson to herself, how complicated life is. She sighs again as she snuggles into the eiderdown. She floats far beyond the exhausting details of daughters and weddings, and her features break into wreathing lines of delight. She wriggles her plump little body, and thinks how like her Elizabeth is; so feminine yet such a determined organizer. She has much to learn, but together they, mother and daughter, will triumph, while Mr Adamson initiates Vincent into the mysteries of being a good husband. Dear Proops, he had never stopped being apologetic. If only Vincent makes half so good a husband, Mrs Adamson thinks as she turns the ring on her finger. The diamond flashes at her intimately, Elizabeth's ring is much larger of course, but it hasn't the same quality.

At this moment Vincent is being examined by the doctor of an insurance company, and though very healthy decides that the more he pays in premium, the less likely is anything to go wrong. Mr Adamson is very impressed by the sum for which Vincent insures himself. He shakes him very warmly by the hand. A nice chap, thinks Vincent.

'It was very good of you to take the trouble over the ring,' he says.

'It was a pleasure, my dear boy,' answers Mr Adamson, 'a real pleasure'.

That afternoon Elizabeth drinks tea in a little green tea-room a few minutes from the centre of Bond Street. She holds her tea-cup between two fingers and describes the final alterations in her wedding-dress. Elaine listens, cheeks glowing. To think of old Dumpy married! Just fancy her leaving in a car on her husband's arm. Her husband. Elizabeth blushes and looks away.

'Which hotel will you stay at?' Elaine asks. 'I mean, you won't leave at once for your . . . holiday?'

'Not likely,' says Elizabeth. 'I've made Vincent get theatre tickets for the evening.' She pours more tea for both of them, holding the tea-pot confidently, her ring-finger displayed to the entire room. She is gratified by the whispering of waitresses standing by the trays of tiny pastries just behind her.

'It really is a lovely stone,' says Elaine. 'Vincent must be terribly in love with you.'

'Isn't it?' answers Elizabeth happily.

It was not until after dinner that evening, after the Adamsons and Vincent had arranged and re-arranged the seating in the cars some seven times, that any of them noticed what had happened. They had all eaten the excellent dinner with jokes and laughter and little reminiscences of Elizabeth's baby-days.

Then Mrs Adamson had turned the talk to serious matters,

and once again the sheets of note-paper with the groupings of aunts and great-aunts, uncles and cousins, were produced and shuffled. It was a discussion which always caused a certain amount of heat, but after an hour it was decided that Mrs Adamson's original arrangement was the best.

'A pity about Uncle Alfred though,' murmured Mr Adamson. 'He was very good to me over the Dickinson-Murdock business.'

'Now don't start arguing all over again dear,' answered Mrs Adamson in a voice forbidding argument. And then she noticed.

She was silent for several moments, staring, her always too prominent eyes popping like a high-bred Pekinese. Then in a voice high-pitched and cracked with shock she cried, 'Elizabeth!'

Elizabeth, dreaming girlishly, looked up blankly. Mr Adamson and Vincent stopped drawing on their Panatellas.

'Elizabeth,' cried Mrs Adamson, 'What have you been up to?' The young couple blushed in harmony. 'Look at your ring-finger, you silly girl,' shrieked Mrs Adamson.

As Elizabeth raised her pale face, tears welled from her eyes.

'Where is it gone?' cried Mrs Adamson again.

'What is the matter, my love?' asked Mr Adamson.

'What's up, Mum?' asked Vincent anxiously.

'Her beautiful diamond—it's gone!' shouted Mrs Adamson.

When they had soothed Elizabeth they retraced all her movements that afternoon.

'You might have eaten it,' suggested Vincent, 'in a jam tart . . .'

'They were éclairs,' said Elizabeth miserably.

'To think a daughter of mine could be so careless,' reiterated

Mrs Adamson. But Mr Adamson just said that he had arranged the insurance at the time it was bought. He seemed quite pleased. He with his skill could recoup such losses. Often with a profit. Jolly good show. Not to worry. There was something to be said, after all, for being a man.

THE BLOTTIK MONOPOLY

IT WAS sure to happen in the end. Ever since the final antique boom in the 1960's dealers had been telling one another it would happen. Regularly every five years someone wrote to the newspapers and complained that 'the Nation's heritage is being shipped for a mess of potage.' The National Trust might save an old house or two but what could it do as mansion after castle, country house after quaint old cottage, all slipped their roots and went, piece by piece, to foreign parts with harder currencies, there to languish thoroughly out of place among fruit trees and swimming-pools and endless sunshine.

But quite apart from the major antique losses—all the minor items were exhausted. Georgian silver, of course, had long since ceased to exist. Sheffield plate was hoarded by a few misers in remote parts of the country. Chelsea and Bow porcelain, Worcester, Swansea and Rockingham—the only pieces ever seen were items imported from the Meissen factories in Alaska (to where they had long ago been removed). Victorian lustres— why, a pair catalogued in very bold type brought 1,700 guineas at Christies and then there was nearly a thousand pounds in the knock-out. Wedgwood (it goes without saying) had been exhausted years ago. What was left? What was there for a dealer to live on?

They, those once sleek and prosperous dealers, used to hang about in disorderly groups outside the empty auction rooms, waiting for the auctioneer to call out to whoever was next on the strict rota of subscribing buyers, the item (a broken bit of Woolworth glass or an old doorstop) it was his privilege to buy. As soon as the fortunate bidder received it, the starving dealers would mob him. That miserable item then changed hands perhaps fifty times, eventually resting in the shooting-brake of the inevitable American dealer always patiently waiting at hand.

The Antique Dealers' Aid Society had, in the early days of the great antique drought, started a fund for fallen dealers, but very quickly it was found that the dealers' enemy was not starvation but inertia. In one year alone (the year when the last bowl of wax fruit caused that riot at Sotheby's) two hundred and sixty-three members of the Association were certified insane. The cause was always the same—loss of vocation. Nothing to buy, nothing to sell. They couldn't stand it, so that the old ones died off like flies while the younger ones took to arson or robbery with violence. The Delinquent Dealer became a major problem of the day.

It was just after mounted police had been forced to break up a mass-meeting of dealers in Hyde Park (they were attempting to tear down the wrought-iron gates to make up an export order) that Morris Blottik (whose vast showrooms in Piccadilly had long ago been converted into an army surplus store) discovered the pan business.

Blottik was a fastidious connoisseur who had, throughout the bad times, kept away from the less reputable groups of dealers. He had scraped a living dealing in respectable goods such as old clothes, bottles, and scrap iron, though only the choicest examples. His thoughts were never far from the historic problem of the antique trade.

'Must those who understand ivory, rot among old bones?' he would suddenly ask the ragged dealers in the Association's soup kitchen. No one answered as he savagely tore a dry baigel to pieces. Everyone was tired of dealer's rant. What was Blottik complaining about? At least he was a respectable rag-and-bone man. What about those poor hunted devils in St James's? How could they know that this very Blottik was to be the saviour of the antique trade?

It happened quite casually, as most important things do. From the days of his glory when he was exporting his ten thousand pounds-worth of goods a week, Blottik retained his habit of retiring to the bathroom for an hour each day. Undisturbed, he would ponder life's problems; when he left for the barrow his careful mind would be soothed. It so happened that one day Blottik had trundled his barrow about the London streets with an unusual feeling of malaise. True, he was intensely preoccupied with the antique problem—but then, he always was. He hastened home and repaired to the bathroom.

Blottik had an early Victorian house in Gunnersbury. The empty rooms echoed to his footsteps as he sped up the stairs. As he opened the bathroom door he had a sense that the moment was one of historic importance. He stood for several seconds as if changed to stone. Then he turned and ran to fetch his toolbox. It took him two hours to prise the lavatory pan free. He phoned an associate and two minutes later was in possession of orders for five hundred decorated basins at £22 a piece. Blottik was a proud man. He was back in the antique business.

Now it was that Blottik's experience told. He did not run about shouting to the wind that he was back in business. No. He had some cards printed, reading:

BOURNE HOLLINGSWORTH
Councillor
Sanitary Cttee.

And he made an arrangement with a little plumber around the corner. Then, one dark night, after having carefully checked to see that no vagrant members of the trade were following him,

Blottik and the plumber set out on what was to be the most important buying trip of modern times.

Blottik's method was simple. He would call at a promising house and present his card.

'I'd like to inspect your w.c.,' he would say. 'I'm from the Council, you know—Sanitary—you don't mind?'

And by this time he would already be glancing into the bathroom. If the toilet was suitably decorated, 'George, bring your tools,' he called out to the plumber. 'We're giving you a brand new toilet,' Blottik explained to the householder, 'the old one's finished—it's an antique.'

By the time George had taken out the old pan and put in a new one Blottik's stock had cost him six pounds apiece, and, as in all good business deals, everyone was satisfied.

What pandemonium there was when the news of Blottik's shipments leaped out! The trade fell over itself to buy from him. At once toilets began to be graded—transfer decorated, polychrome—solid body—lead-glazed—and, of course, all the famous old masters of basin moulding were listed. Pilkington's Soundless—Beal's Ferrara—Master's Milady, Henry's Invictus. The names are famous today among collectors.

America went mad for the line. Toilet pans were seen all over New York, adapted as hot or cool air vents, set in gilded frames (maker's name foremost), garnished with flowers and trailing ferns. *Vogue* devoted six pages to the more *chic* of what was now called 'the basin-maker's art.' It was wonderful while it lasted.

Of course it was only a flash in the pan. Within three years there wasn't a fine old toilet to be found in the British Isles. But Blottik was firmly established as an expert and his book, *Famous Basins*, was a collector's *vade mecum*. In those mad months a number of dealers had become solvent and a few of the more conservative ones had died of chagrin, but now once again the wild dangerous groups were beginning to gather outside the empty auction rooms. The recurrent crisis was again imminent.

Blottik himself, the dwindling traders felt, should have at least been knighted, because, although the end of business was again at hand, wasn't Britain the only welfare state in the world where every house had a fine new w.c?

EIGHT YEARS IN THE MAKING

Mrs toshak was forty-two when she first saw the archangel
Michael at an auction-rooms off Bond Street. She knew his
name was Michael for the auctioneer called it as he made a
note of the fact that a small collection of cracked Greek pots
had changed hands. And she could see at once that he must be
an archangel for he was nearly six and a half feet tall, and his
classical features were set in a pale skin and topped with a
growth of closely-curled golden hair. He for his part—being
older than he looked and admiring Mrs Toshak's experienced
figure as much as the encrustations of diamonds about her
person—remarked to himself that there was much of the un-
tamed gipsy in this still elegant lady who watched him in so
predatory a manner.

Now to tell the truth, Mrs Toshak was an Armenian carpet-
dealer's wife who had come to London by way of Smyrna,
Budapest and Paris, where Toshak himself had had the decency
to die after taking out a very sizeable insurance policy with a
gullible English company. Thence London, in the area of
Sloane Street—with a small elegant shop in gilt and black and
stripes, hung with dubious landscapes of blotched satyrs and
forced nymphs. Mrs Toshak was an interior decorator. She
could at a glance tell just how well Michael would fit in to her
décor and business. As an experienced dealer, she could sense
almost to the pound his precise market price.

The archangel Michael, for his part, was a recent importa-
tion from Vienna. His sponsor, a collector of Spanish baroque
furniture, had picked him up in a café in the Ringstrasse and
had recognized immediately how well he would tone with the

baroque. As a valet Michael had left nothing to be desired, but his employer, who had at first been quite enchanted by his man's innate sense of the aesthetic, began to worry at the gaps in his collection of Hispano-Mauresque plates. A dealer from whom he was about to buy one of his own pieces was stupid enough to mention an Austrian count who had sold it to him. 'Was he six foot six tall and blond?' asked the collector. Michael and his employer parted company that same afternoon. The employer sighed for a week or so and then found a new valet through a fellow collector. And Michael found himself, without surprise, in the fine art business.

Thus it was then that Mrs Toshak and Michael met in the pursuit of business at the very heart of the heartless world of their refined trade. Michael turned to leave the rooms after his last purchase, a slight sneer wrinkling his lips. He always bore in mind the fact that in the not far distant future he would be buying for much more than shillings, and he was cultivating a bidding manner suited to the higher levels of dealing. Mrs Toshak cut across his exit swift as a dark cobra, and the two drew level at the swing-doors.

'The last lot—you bought?' inquired Mrs Toshak with a hard glitter in her eyes showing to advantage against the velvet of her voice.

'That is so, madam,' replied Michael, making his words drip slowly with tenderness. 'But surely—it must be—but no, how could it—it is the Princess von Dorfensleben. My dear Princess, enchanted,' and he stooped low to kiss Mrs Toshak's hand.

Although Mrs Toshak could not resist a smile of amusement at Michael's methods, she was forced to admire the ease with which he fell into so patent a lie. In this way he was like her own dead Florio—a man capable of selling a silk Bokhara every day of the week. But so tall, so blond, so aristocratic.

She introduced herself and enjoyed Michael's apologies for a minute or two. Then she returned to the matter in hand.

'Come to my shop at six with this rubbish you have bought,' Mrs Toshak ordered, and with a scintillating wave of her fingers she leapt into a taxi, leaving Michael to smile indiscriminately at the street.

In spite of his willingness to wait upon events with the same devotedness he had shown as a valet, Michael was a little perplexed by his new friend. With mixed feelings but with a delicious sense of anticipation he drew up at Mrs Toshak's shop front, a discreet affair of gold and black cupidons surmounted by white brocade drapes with tassels everywhere. He entered, walking reverently upon the black carpet, his eyes turned down modestly as Mrs Toshak came towards him from the shadowed depth of the room. They had hardly time to exchange the courtesies appropriate to such a meeting when the door opened again and in came Mrs Toshak's expected clients—a portly gentleman with white moustaches, and a lady elegantly dressed as only a woman past her second youth need be.

Mrs Toshak glided forward to greet them like a *grande dame* afflicted with the intimate huskiness of a brothel madam. She introduced them to Michael by his full title, and then as they looked together at a superb chandelier, she whispered to Michael, 'Sell her the Greeks—he is mine.' With the formal politeness of an old dance the four then paired off, Michael telling the lady of the glory that is still to be found in Greece. 'O Athens,' said the lady, 'O Sparta—I've never been to Greece. How lovely.' For Michael had led from the general discussion to the particular pots he had to offer.

When it was all over, Mrs Toshak and Michael looked at each other. Their faces were flushed and their eyes swam. Mrs Toshak put out her hand and Michael's slipped a cheque into it. Then together they breathed, 'Three hundred and seventy pounds.' A moment later Mrs Toshak had clasped Michael to her breast. He settled with her for a hundred and fifty. Only at one point in the discussion it seemed that a promising relationship was in danger. But he looked at her with a sudden, poignant expression of regret in his eyes. Her heart melted like the polar cap of the earth enjoying the first heat in its history. He got his hundred and fifty in cash.

Mrs Toshak is now fifty. Michael is a little stouter, and he wears glasses. Many are the killings they have enjoyed together, Mrs Toshak confidently directing, Michael leaping into the battle like a Prussian Guards officer and winning golden commissions every week. Soon he will be earning enough to keep himself in the style to which his employer has accustomed him —and a little later on, perhaps, he will be able to steal enough from Mrs Toshak to buy a full half-share in her prosperous business.